MAN
OVERBOARD

A CRIME CLUB SELECTION

A glamorous South American widow was the lure that drew Don Kendrick to board the *Duchess of Malfi,* but when he offered the deck steward a sizable tip to let him know if either of the lady's deck companions fell overboard he did not expect events to make a prophet of him. When one of these gentlemen did disappear, Don had to answer some very embarrassing questions. Later, when another disappearance, on dry land this time, pointed the finger at him, Don felt that he had followed glamour too fast and too far into real danger.

Scene: Atlantic Ocean, British Isles, English Channel

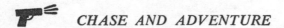 *CHASE AND ADVENTURE*

MAN OVERBOARD

Allan MacKinnon

PUBLISHED FOR THE CRIME CLUB BY
DOUBLEDAY & COMPANY, INC., GARDEN CITY, NEW YORK
1965

All of the characters in this book are fictitious, fortunately, and any resemblance to actual persons, living or dead, would be a big surprise to the author.

To
JACK HOUSE
after all these years—
Slaintè!

MAN
OVERBOARD

The Foreign Secretary frowned at his weekend host and said, "Dammit, Hugh, I think I'd better not hear any more."

"But this is off the record—for your own ear only."

"In my job," said the Minister, "nothing's for my own ear only. I have a duty to the P.M. and the Cabinet; and if I happen to learn that certain British business interests contemplate action likely to cause trouble with Washington or the O.A.S. . . . well . . ." He shrugged, and looked out of the window at the peaceful Sussex countryside.

His host smiled rather sardonically and said, "Sorry, Jeff. I'm basically dishonest myself, but I think I understand how you feel. You can't be both a statesman and an old school chum, and it's not fair to ask you to try. But are you willing to answer one question? I'll make it hypothetical."

"If I can."

"Let me lay a foundation for it, then. And while I'm doing so we might lay a foundation for lunch as well." He rose, poured out two glasses of sherry, and said, "Under Simon Bolivar, as you no doubt know, the north-western countries of South America were a single republic called Greater Colombia. Then came the separatist movements that ended with Venezuela and Ecuador peeling off to become self-governing states. Later, with U.S. instigation and support, Panama revolted and did the same. Now, then—my question. If this tradition of separatism should suddenly produce another successful split in that part of the world, would Britain give diplomatic recognition to the breakaway republic? And, if so, how quickly?"

The Foreign Secretary sighed. "My dear Hugh," he said, "the Monroe Doctrine—"

"Lays down that there shall be no European interference in the internal affairs of American nations, such as taking sides in a revolution. Quite so. I'm not asking you for the Royal Marines or even for money. I'm only asking how Britain would react if part of a certain petroleum-producing country—the part with the oilfields in it, naturally—should pull out and set up house on its own."

His guest eyed him thoughtfully for a few moments, and then said, "You know, I suppose, what world opinion was on the U.S. role in that Panamanian breakaway?"

"Certainly. Almost universal condemnation, so strong that eventually the Yanks paid Colombia heavy damages. But I've already told you that nobody's asking Britain, as such, to back anything. This hypothetical breakaway would be the spontaneous uprising of a freedom-loving people under a popular national hero."

"Who, once he was in the saddle, might inexplicably start giving preference to British oil interests instead of U.S. and Dutch ones?"

The host grinned. "I cannot exclude that possibility," he admitted.

"In such an event," said the Minister carefully, "I imagine that Her Majesty's Government might extend fairly prompt recognition to the new republic—provided, of course, that nobody was able to pin anything on the said British oil interests, and let the Monroe Doctrine rear its ugly head." He smiled suddenly. "They don't call us *perfide Albion* for nothing, Hugh . . . This really is excellent sherry."

ONE

With no suspicion that he might have embarked on something much bigger than a mere Atlantic crossing, Donald Kendrick came out of his cabin and ascended to the *Duchess of Malfi*'s glass-enclosed Promenade Deck.

Only a few pre-breakfast strollers were about, but already the long lines of lounge-chairs, each with its leg-rest, cushions and neatly folded rug, lay ready for use. He worked his way methodically aft along the port side, reading the name-cards. The name he sought was not there.

On the open after-deck he paused for a time, watching his native Canada glide past. It was Saturday, September 20, and the distant shore was a patchwork of fall colours—reds bright and dark, warm browns and delicate yellows, all set against the green of grass that had been rained on overnight. The still waters of the St. Lawrence glinted in the sun, disturbed only where the liner's bulbous bow nosed through them, and he thought how pleasant it would be if this kind of weather held all the way to the Clyde; pleasant but, with an equinox at hand, unlikely. He set off forward again, reading the name-cards on the starboard side.

And there it was, almost right away: *Sra. M. Gomez, Cabin U9*. The chair was flanked by those of Mr. W. Hadley, Cabin M36, and Mr. F. Farrell, U7. Kendrick memorized the men's names and went off in search of the Deck Steward.

Yes, said the steward with an approving eye on the ten-dollar bill between Kendrick's fingers, it was often possible to arrange a transfer of chairs. Which one did he want?

"Either Mr. Hadley's or Mr. Farrell's, I don't mind which," said Kendrick. "They're down aft on this side."

The steward consulted a notebook and his face fell. "Not a hope, sir," he said gloomily. "I remember the gentlemen now. They both particularly asked for chairs next to the señora. If only you'd come to me before we left Montreal . . ."

"I wasn't on board," said Kendrick. "I joined the ship last night, at Quebec. Ah, well! If we can't work a swap, that's that." Deftly he switched the ten-spot for a single, which he held out. "If either of them falls overboard, or anything, this buys me an option on his chair."

Idly, as he made his way below decks to breakfast, he wondered who Hadley and Farrell might be. The latter's cabin, from its number, must be next door to the lady's. Accident, or design? Officially, he knew, Manuela Gomez was travelling alone, but the official is not always the actual.

There was no sign of her at breakfast, and it was nearly eleven before he saw her. When he did he caught his breath, for she was even more beautiful, in her classical Spanish way, than he had realized. Moreover her figure, as displayed by a sun-halter, and her long legs, as set off by short shorts, transcended criticism. She was about five foot six, he guessed, and, give or take a year, the same age as himself—twentyseven.

She was on the Promenade Deck, stitching some intricate embroidery on what looked like a blouse, and chatting animatedly with what looked like an Empire-building Englishman in the mid-thirties, who sat on the Hadley chair. Kendrick watched them for a few moments; but when you are a broad-shouldered six foot one, weighing 198 lb net, it is difficult to stand around inconspicuously. He climbed to the Hurricane Deck and watched the river traffic instead.

Here, within minutes, he fell prey to a talkative priest called Maguire, who had sat next to him at breakfast, and apparently considered that this made them indissociable travelling companions for the trip. The man still had him in tow when the gongs sounded for lunch.

There was again no sign of Manuela Gomez in the room, which was puzzling, for the *Duchess* was a one-class vessel and there was no other restaurant. Maybe she retained that superb shape by avoiding temptation and eating low-calorie sludge in solitude. But there was no sign of the Empire-building Hadley either.

After lunch Kendrick shook off the garrulous Father, went to his cabin, sat down on his capacious bunk and gave himself over to thought. Without boorishly crashing a duo, who may for all you know be old friends or even more, how do you make a woman's acquaintance aboard ship?

The day's Programme of Events lay on the writing-table, and he searched it for ideas. There would be a Get-Together Dance in the evening, he saw, but he had a hunch that, quite apart from any claim Hadley might have on her company, the señora would be one of the major targets at it. Something less competitive was called for. He frowned at the Programme, and suddenly saw the answer: 2.30 p.m. BOAT MUSTER.

There were detailed instructions (by cabin blocks) for reaching one's allotted lifeboat station, and he saw with pleasure that Hadley's M36, like his own M20, was on the port side, whereas U9's was on the starboard. He noted the route to it, found his life-jacket at the bottom of the wardrobe, and sat down patiently to wait.

Promptly at half-past two the ship's whistle and a flock of alarm bells sounded off. At three the muster was dismissed, and Kendrick said to nobody in particular, "This boat-drill gets you survival-minded, doesn't it?" Nobody replied, so he turned to his immediate neighbour and said, "How's about going down to the pool and brush up on our swimming, Mrs. Gomez?"

The girl's eyes widened in what, for a moment, looked like fright. "I—have we met?" she asked.

"We have now. Kendrick's my name—Don Kendrick."

"But how did you know mine?"

Kendrick smiled slightly. "As soon as you left your deck-chair this morning," he said, "I ran along and read it on the card. Then I found out which boat station you had, and here I am. It was the only way I could figure of getting to talk to you without that other guy around."

The tension on her lovely face had eased a little, but she still eyed him cautiously. "And why did you want to talk to me, señor?" she asked.

Kendrick shrugged. "I could be mysterious, I suppose," he said, "and offer you three guesses. Or I could lie, and say I'm taking a Gallup Poll on something. Or I could come right out with the truth—that it's because you're easily the most beautiful woman on board, and I'm only human." He grinned as disarmingly as he could. "Now snub me."

She studied his face for a moment, then showed her perfect teeth in a smile. "I'll reserve judgement," she said.

After their swim they went up to the Ducal Lounge for tea; over which they made the not unusual discovery that, although Kendrick had visited the lady's native Colombia, and she had spent some time in Canada, they had not one acquaintance in common. Then he escorted her to her chair on the Promenade Deck. Hadley, looking rather disgruntled, acknowledged the girl's introduction; and Kendrick, in the continued absence of the other flanker, sat on F. Farrell's chair and chatted sociably.

Hadley, it appeared, was a radio engineer, homebound after a spell on loan to the C.B.C., and glad to be so. "It's not that I don't like Canada, old boy, but—well, it's such a youthful country. There's a kind of calm maturity about England that's really much more restful."

On the point of questioning the calm maturity associated with the Beatles and the Dave Clark Five, Kendrick heard a harsh and unfriendly voice saying, "Pardon me, but you got my seat."

"Sorry," said Kendrick, rising. The newcomer was a keg-necked bruiser in the fifties, with a crew cut and a red, bad-tempered face. "I noticed it was vacant for the moment, so—"

"You rent these things for money," barked Mr. Farrell, and sat down heavily. Kendrick withdrew.

Casually questioned, the girl had told him that both men were strangers to her, and she did not seem to suspect that either had landed beside her otherwise than by chance. Why Hadley had bribed the Deck Steward was pretty obvious; but surely a man of Farrell's age couldn't seriously fancy his chances? Maybe, of course, he merely wanted to feast his eyes and have himself a day-dream. It didn't seem to matter very much.

What did matter was that Kendrick was now on reasonably informal terms with her, and also that he had solved the mystery of her non-appearance at meals. She and Hadley attended an overspill Second Sitting. It was as simple as that. He decided to match his timetable to theirs.

At six-thirty, while the Main Sitting swarmed into the restaurant, he buttonholed the Chief Steward and asked for a transfer to the later service. This arranged, he returned to his cabin. A large man, bending over the writing-table, swung round as he entered, and gaped at him. It was F. Farrell.

"Looking for something?" Kendrick asked pleasantly.

"I—I—Holy cow! Is this your room?"

"Yeah. Yours is U7. Upper Deck, not Main."

The big red face became redder. "I never thought this was my room," Farrell grated. "Ya think I don't know which floor I'm on? I thought this room belonged to a guy I know, and I came in to leave a note for him. I coulda swore he told me he had M30."

"Probably he did. This is M20."

Farrell looked at him incredulously. "Ya got to be kidding," he said.

Kendrick pulled the door fully open and pointed to the little numberplate on the outside. The other peered at it, then gave a

shame-faced smile. "Darned if y'ain't right," he said. "My wife's
been nagging me for years to get glasses, but . . . Gee I'm
sorry, Mr.—uh?"

"Kendrick. Donald Kendrick."

"Mine's Frank Farrell. Gosh, I do apologise."

"Forget it," said Kendrick affably, ushering him out. "I'll do
the same for you some time." He closed the door on Farrell's
puzzled expression and turned to the writing-table. His passport
lay in the middle of it, though he was almost certain he had left
it in the drawer. Almost. Not quite.

His baggage did not seem to have been disturbed, but of
course Farrell could have been in the room for only a few minutes at most. And, equally of course, the man's story just might
have been true. To myopic eyes the figure 2 would quite possibly resemble a 3, and the passport . . . the more Kendrick
thought about the passport the less sure he was that he had not
left it on the table himself. Nevertheless . . .

The Get-Together Dance proved a most enjoyable affair; but
Bill Hadley, predictably, hung around Manuela like an aura,
and Kendrick was glad he had not waited until now to make
her acquaintance. He decided to give himself an evening off;
scanned the crowded ballroom in search of suitable company;
then closed in on a plump little blonde in a tight frock with a
distracting neckline. She turned out to like large Canadians,
and after a time agreed to join him in exploring the unlit Sun
Deck. There they Got Together very pleasantly indeed.

Kendrick was at the Purser's Bureau at opening time on
Sunday, and learned with no great surprise that M30 was a
double-berth room, at present shared by two ladies from Leeds.

So Frank Farrell was a liar, and had known perfectly well
which cabin he was in; and had quite reasonably believed,
moreover, that he would be undisturbed in it for the duration of
the Main Sitting. But to what end? Maybe the simplest thing
would be to find him and ask him.

The man was in his deck-chair, but dozens of other people

were in theirs, and it was obviously no time for a showdown. Kendrick strolled on, slap into the welcoming clutches of Father Maguire, whose virtual monologue ended only when his audience escaped to the Protestant Service in the ballroom. By no means a regular churchgoer ashore, Kendrick never missed a service when he happened to be afloat, nor failed to raise his sturdy baritone in the traditional hymn *For those in peril on the sea.* For one thing, he liked the tune; and for another, it seemed like a prudent time to sing it.

After lunch he decided to have a last, long look at his country before it went below the horizon. The sheltered waters of the Gulf were now far behind them, and in the narrow Strait of Belle Isle the *Duchess* had already been riding the Atlantic swell. She was still doing so, but harder. Kendrick went down aft, and found a fair-sized gathering, all gazing astern with varying degrees of emotion.

That's Canada, that was, he thought, looking at the low-lying island on the port quarter. Canada, yes; but he was a West Coast man, and Belle Isle was about twice as far from there as it was from England. A big place, Canada . . . He saw Farrell standing alone by the rail, and walked over to join him.

"Made any more unfortunate mistakes lately?" he asked in a conversational tone.

Farrell looked at him with apparent bewilderment. "What the heck are you talking about?" he queried.

"Your boy friend in M30. Did you know that the whimsical fellow had registered as a brace of dames? Or didn't you care enough to check, and think up another story?"

Farrell was frowning at him. "You some kind of a nut?" he demanded. Heads were turning away from the view to watch the two big men by the rail.

"No," said Kendrick mildly, "merely a guy with some natural curiosity. I wondered why you were snooping in my room yesterday. Care to—"

"Hold it, bub!" The older man's face was flushed, but his pale eyes were ice. He clenched his enormous fists and said, "That's slander. I was never in your goddam room in my life, and if you say I was I'll clobber you before I sue. So—mind your step, is all." He turned on his heel and strode away. Kendrick watched him go, then shrugged, and resumed his contemplation of the receding land.

It had just disappeared when the plump little blonde found him, and dragged him off to play the time-honoured deck games of jack quoits and bullboard. These were followed in due course by cocktails; which in turn were followed by dinner and, as soon as it was dark enough, by further deck games of an equally time-honoured but rather more private nature.

Next morning the weather was distinctly lively. They were well out in the Atlantic now, and the swell had increased to what even a sailor would have called "moderate"; which, by landlubbing standards, is pretty fierce. The *Duchess* rolled, and the wind strengthened, and the *Duchess* pitched, for wind and swell were coming from different quarters. Scores of passengers, including Mrs. Gomez, took to their bunks, and the ship's surgeon was kept busy giving anti-seasickness injections.

Deck games in the dark were going to be somewhat draughty, Kendrick thought, and he wondered whether he could coax the little blonde out of the minor league and into his cabin instead. The situation, however, did not arise. By nightfall she had somehow met the dashing Third Officer, and her expression indicated that she would now be out of circulation till the *Duchess* docked. Kendrick went to the ship's cinema by himself. The film was punk.

By breakfast-time on Tuesday the full meaning of the term "equinoctial gale" had become manifest, and the restaurant was pitifully empty. The wind was Force 9, and even the ship's log classed the swell as "heavy" and called the sea "very rough." What the passengers called it would have filled a book with vigorous, colourful prose. Twenty-five thousand tons gross register may look fairly solid in print, and even in port, but it's a ping pong ball in mid-Atlantic.

After a somewhat boring day spent largely in dodging Father Maguire, Kendrick remembered that the unlucky in love are proverbially lucky at cards, and decided that his loss of the blonde entitled him to make a real killing if he could locate a poker game somewhere that evening.

He found one in the smokeroom on the Boat Deck and, despite the fact that Frank Farrell was of the company, had a very enjoyable session. For the proverb proved true, and he felt that he ought to buy the Third Officer a drink some time.

About eleven-thirty Farrell yawned unconvincingly and said, "That's me for tonight, boys. Guess I'll get a breath of air and then hit the sack."

On an impulse Kendrick said, "Me too, if nobody minds. Except for the breath of air, maybe—it's going past too fast tonight. Anyone wants his money back, I'll be here same time tomorrow. Okay?" The players agreed and dispersed.

Farrell had been glancing unobtrusively at his watch during the last few hands, so it was long odds, Kendrick felt, that he had an appointment—and a surreptitious one at that, for surely no normal person would go out on the open, windswept deck for pleasure. It was now the snooper's turn to be snooped on, he decided; gave the man a few seconds' start, and then followed.

Outside, conditions were even worse than he had expected. The dimly lit deck was slippery with recent rain, and a spray-laden, sledgehammer gust sent him sliding helplessly backwards to slam into the angle of a deckhouse. Rubbing salt water from his eyes, he peered both ways through the gloom, and spotted his man. Farrell was going up a narrow companionway that led to the Sun Deck, and he was not alone. He was following someone, someone whose flapping black skirt whipped the big fellow's face, but whose upper half had already gone out of sight. Lurching as the ship bucked, and trying to control his feet on the slick planks, Kendrick clutched at a handrail and pulled himself along the heaving deck in the teeth of the wind.

By the time he reached the companionway both Farrell and his partner had disappeared, and for a moment he had qualms about following. But heck, no, it couldn't be a simple amorous assignation—not out on deck in this weather. He put his foot on the first step, and something exploded in his head with a blaze of fireworks and a surge of pain. The second swipe knocked him cold.

TWO

He came to in bed, in what seemed to be a small, dimly lit
hospital ward—except that hospital beds do not jump, creak,
and fall away from under you. His head was aching, his eyes
were blurred, and for a few moments he thought that that
was why the bed was acting so oddly. Then memory came back.
He was in the *Duchess of Malfi*, of course. This must be the
sick bay, which would account for the hot-water bottles against
his legs. But why was he in it?

More memory came back, and he knew exactly why he was
in it. He had been trying to spy on Frank Farrell and some unknown woman in a black evening dress, and he had been
knocked out. Apparently they had posted a sentry to ensure
privacy for their meeting.

Kendrick raised himself on one elbow and rang the little
bell on the bedside table. A middle-aged nurse came in, walking
as steadily as if the room were standing still, gave him a
friendly smile and said, "How are you?"

"Sore in the head, thank you."

"Yes, you got a very nasty crack. I'll give you a sedative and
you'll probably feel better next time you wake. Doctor will see
you again in the morning."

"Again?"

"He saw you when you were brought in. Don't you remember?"

"I don't. You mean I was conscious?"

"Oh yes, for a minute or two, while we were putting you to

bed. But you obviously wanted to go to sleep, so of course we let you."

"Thanks. Who brought me in, Nurse?"

"Two of the crew. An officer found you shortly after midnight, when he was coming off watch. You must have been blown against a stanchion or something, I suppose."

Kendrick was silent for a time. "I guess so," he said at last. He was too tired at the moment for the kind of questioning the truth would evoke, and too tired also to phrase the truth so that he would not appear as a Peeping Tom.

Next time he woke it was nearly ten o'clock, and the ship's motion, though still sprightly, had abated from its midnight violence. His head felt much better, and he welcomed the breakfast brought him by a day nurse. As she set the tray before him, the ship's whistle and alarm bells sounded urgently. Kendrick raised his eyebrows, and the nurse gave him a reassuring smile. "It's all right," she said. "You're excused."

Kendrick grinned, said, "I just go down with the ship, huh?" and started on the poached eggs.

Later the doctor examined him and pronounced him fit for discharge. "Your bedroom steward has brought your shaving tackle and some clean clothes," he said. "As soon as you're dressed, the Captain would like to see you."

"The Captain?" echoed Kendrick in surprise. "What does he want to see me for?"

"Well," said the doctor, and it struck Kendrick that the man was avoiding his eye, "you've had an accident aboard his ship, you know, and—ah—perhaps he wants to find out if you mean to sue the Line, or—"

"I don't."

"Well, I really can't say what he wants, but he certainly wants you, as soon as you're ready." And the doctor bustled away. All of which, Kendrick thought, was somewhat odd.

A rating was standing by to act as guide, and led him by quiet ways up to the holy of holies overlooking the foredeck.

Captain Nicholson, a compact little man with a weathered face, was what the London shipping offices call "a Storn"—that is, a native of the island of Lewis, which probably exports more deep-sea mariners than any comparable spot on earth. Kendrick had noticed the trace of a Hebridean lilt in his accent during the service on Sunday, and he noticed it again when the Captain directed him to a chair in front of the big desk at which he was seated.

"According to your passport," said the Captain, and Kendrick saw with surprise that it was lying on the desk, "you're a Canadian, born in Vancouver but now resident in the United Kingdom. Your profession is shown as journalist. Correct?"

"Correct. I do a column for the *Sunday Bulletin*."

The Captain nodded. "I don't read that kind of rag myself," he said, "but my steward recognized your name. Right, mister. At my request my London office got in touch with the *Bulletin* this morning, and was told that Donald Kendrick, having recently completed a tour of South America for the paper, is now spending some leave with friends in Montreal." He looked challengingly at the journalist.

Kendrick looked right back at him. *That kind of rag*, indeed. Maybe it was, but who was the Captain to say so? "Yes?" he said politely.

"You've no comment to make?"

"Merely that your information is largely correct. I have just completed a tour, as you can see from my visa pages, and I did spend part of my leave in Montreal; with a Mr. and Mrs. Peter MacLaren, in case London gave you their names. MacLaren's a travel agent, and his wife's my sister. So?"

The Captain eyed him coldly. "The *Bulletin* did give us those names," he admitted, "but they also told us that Kendrick was flying back from Montreal on the thirtieth of the month. This is only the twentyfourth, the *Duchess* isn't an aeroplane, and you didn't come aboard at Montreal. There may be some simple explanation, mister, but if so I want to hear it. Otherwise I can only assume you've got hold of Kendrick's passport and impersonated him for some reason of your own."

Kendrick bit back a curt reply and said, "Has your Montreal office tried checking with the MacLarens to see if I'm still there?"

The Captain ignored the question. "I don't like even minor mysteries aboard my ship," he said, "and I don't propose to have any. If you want to avoid trouble I'd advise you speak up."

The journalist's eyes were blazing, but he knew the dictatorial powers of a ship's master, so he braked his temper as best he could. "It's quite simple," he said shortly. "My sister has three small sons. I was probably tired and edgy after covering thirteen countries and umpteen thousand miles in a few weeks, but anyway I found my nephews driving me nuts. I decided to curtail my visit and get some rest before I went back to work, and I thought a few days aboard ship would be just the prescription. Naturally I didn't want to hurt anyone's feelings, so I said my paper had recalled me and told me to return by sea, so that I could do a piece about life in a liner."

Nicholson nodded non-committally, and Kendrick guessed that he had already received confirmative information from Montreal. "And had you any particular reason for choosing my ship?" asked the Captain.

Kendrick suppressed a grin. He had indeed had a particular reason, but he was quite sure his brother-in-law would not have divulged it to the shipping company. The two had been in Peter MacLaren's office on Friday morning, arranging Kendrick's passage by the *Empress of Britain,* when a vision of loveliness had come in to pick up tickets at the front counter. MacLaren had seen Kendrick's reaction, laughed and said, *"Niña hechicera,* huh?"

"Niña who?"

MacLaren had laughed again and said, "That's not her name, it's Spanish for 'glamour girl'. Her name's Manuela Gomez, she's a South American widow, and she's off to Europe for a holiday. Travelling in the *Duchess of Malfi* all by herself, Don. Don't you wish you were going too?"

"Pete, old buddy," Don had said, "I am."

"No dice. The ship sails in an hour or so, and you haven't even started your packing yet."

"Does it call at Quebec, by any chance?"

"Yeah. Leaves there about eleven tonight."

"With me on board, having made it comfortably overland. You may not know this, Pete, but our Latin cousins guard their women like insane when there are transient *gringos* around. For eight solid weeks I lived on appetizers and stimulants, starving in the midst of plenty; and now here at last is my chance to try for a full course South American meal. A widow, yet! Wow!"

Kendrick came back to the present and said, "Your ship was the first available sailing, Captain. I was too late to catch her in Montreal so I joined her at Quebec."

"Without telling your employers your change of plan?"

"No need. I'm on holiday. And if they did want me back in a hurry they couldn't get me—not while I'm at sea."

The Captain was silent for a long time, and then his hard face seemed to become even harder. "Right!" he said. "Now we come to last night, when you were found unconscious on the Boat Deck. What the devil took you out there at the height of the gale?"

Kendrick looked at him blandly. "Love of fresh air," he said.

The Captain scowled and said, "Don't try to be funny, mister, I don't like it. You went out there looking for a fight, didn't you?"

"I did what?"

"You went—" The desk telephone buzzed quietly, and Nicholson lifted the receiver. "Captain here," he said, and listened for a time. "Right. Thank you. Dismiss the muster and resume normal routine, please."

He cradled the receiver and studied the journalist for a few moments without expression. Then he said, "You had an altercation on Sunday with a Montreal private detective named Farrell. Witnesses state that he threatened you with violence. Last night Farrell left a card party at eleven-thirtytwo and went out on deck. Seconds later you followed him. I suggest that that was by arrangement—that he and you had agreed to settle your differences at a time and place where you'd be safe from interruption."

"That," said Kendrick, "is very wide of the mark. Farrell didn't even know I was following him. He had arranged to meet somebody, all right, but it wasn't me, it was a woman. Ask him."

"Unfortunately I can't."

"No? I thought a Captain's autocratic powers entitled—"

"My autocratic powers, mister, don't enable me to question somebody who's not aboard my ship."

Kendrick stared at him, only half comprehending what he had heard.

"At seven o'clock this morning," Nicholson continued grimly, "his bedroom steward noted that Farrell hadn't slept in his own room. Well, that's no novelty at sea, for passengers often seem to leave their morals at home. But when he didn't appear at breakfast—the first meal he'd missed—and we couldn't find anyone who'd seen him since last night, I had a search started. Then I ordered the extra boat drill, which emptied such staterooms as we hadn't been able to check before, and my Staff Commander phoned me a minute ago to report the result. Frank Farrell is definitely no longer aboard the ship. You, on your own admission, were the last person to see him alive. And as far back as Saturday morning you said something to the Deck Steward about the possibility of Farrell's going overboard. At the time, the man thought you were joking."

There was a very long silence indeed. At last Kendrick said, "I had no idea Farrell was a private eye . . . I suppose your theory is that he and I were enemies back in Montreal, that I learned he was going to take this trip, and that I made a pier-head jump in order to take it too, with the sole purpose of tipping him over the side? And that the moment I'd done it I got blown against a stanchion, and stunned?"

The Captain gave a frosty little smile. "I can't say I'd worked it out in quite such detail," he said. "Is that what happened?"

"No," said Kendrick, "this is what happened." He told the whole story, from his surprising Farrell in the cabin, viâ the "altercation" on Sunday, to the moment when he had been blackjacked on the Boat Deck. Long before he ended, Captain Nicholson was registering frank disbelief.

"You certainly have the journalistic imagination, mister," he said, somehow contriving to make *journalistic* sound like a dirty word. "But I'm afraid your first story was much more convincing. Anyway, we'll be in the Clyde in fortyeight hours or so, and after that the police can thrash it out. Meantime, you'll be confined to your cabin. And you're lucky you're not in irons."

The fuming Kendrick was locked in his cabin by the Master-at-arms and told that lunch would be sent in at one o'clock. By the time it arrived he had calmed down considerably, for he had realized what excellent copy this experience would make when it was all over. Many a columnist, he reflected, had tried to find some new slant on the conventional "transatlantic crossing" stuff, but none that he could recall had ever been able to give a prisoner's-eye view of the voyage.

After lunch he uncased his typewriter and, trying to accommodate himself to the ship's motion, hammered out the rough draft of a few paragraphs on the subject. He was thus engaged when a petty officer arrived with the news that Captain Nicholson wished to see him right away.

Captain Nicholson sat at his desk, looking as if there was nobody he less wished to see. He frowned at Kendrick for a full half minute and then said, "You visited Colombia in the course of your South American tour, didn't you?"

"I did."

"What were you doing there?"

Kendrick raised his eyebrows. "The same thing I was doing everywhere else," he said. "Talking to people, looking at things and places, gathering material for an article."

"Get involved with a woman at all?"

"No. Why?"

"Farrell tried to pump your bedroom steward about you on Saturday afternoon. Said he'd seen a Bogotà hotel label on one of your suitcases while it was outside your cabin door, and wanted to know how long you'd been in the country and what you'd been doing there. Seemed pretty excited, the steward says."

"And when the steward couldn't help him, he went in to see what he could discover for himself?"

"Apparently, if your story about catching him there is true. I thought he might have been—you know, private detective— looking for hotel bills or the like. Divorce evidence."

"I'm not married and I wasn't fooling around."

"Don't suppose it matters," Nicholson grunted, and then he fell silent for so long that the journalist began to fidget. "Er— Kendrick," he said at last, using that form of address for the first time, "I've been thinking it over, and—and I've decided that perhaps it's not strictly necessary to keep you locked up after all." The words seemed to have been dragged from him like teeth without benefit of anaesthesia.

"You mean I'm at large again?"

The Captain nodded unhappily. "Till the Scottish police come aboard," he said. Then he squared his shoulders and scowled. "But if in the meantime," he snapped, with a return of his former fire, "you feel inclined to cheat the hangman by going over the side, my Bo'sun has instructions to provide you with any chains and weights you may want." He made a gesture of dismissal, and Kendrick left.

It was not difficult, he thought as he made his way to the passenger area of the ship, to explain the Captain's ostensible change of mind. He was still the supreme authority while at sea, of course, but no officer interested in retaining his command will willingly go against his owners' wishes if he can avoid it. It seemed probable to Kendrick that the top brass of the Webster Line—more afraid of bad publicity, perhaps, than was the old Storn—had considered it poor policy to lock up a columnist whose "rag" had a five million circulation, on any grounds short of a cast-iron case. The climb-down had obviously broken Nicholson's heart, but presumably he liked to eat.

Kendrick went straight to the Purser's Bureau and despatched two radio-telegrams, one to Peter MacLaren in Montreal, the other to the *Bulletin*'s News Editor in London. Then he went to U Deck, found Manuela's stewardess, and enquired after the young widow's health.

Mrs. Gomez, said the stewardess, had been so unwell the night before that the ship's surgeon had prescribed a king size sedative, which had been administered hypodermically by a nurse. The stewardess had stood by till the drug worked, and had looked in again shortly before midnight, to find the widow still out for the count. Manuela, in fact, had not come alive until mid-morning, but had then done so feeling considerably better. She had brunched lightly, had managed to retain the food, and half an hour ago had ventured up on deck.

The news pleased Kendrick for two reasons, the less obvious being that it dispelled a vague suspicion he had had about the wearer of that black evening frock. On the face of it, it seemed likely that the private detective had been murdered by somebody he was on board to investigate, and that he had been decoyed to the killing-ground by a woman accomplice. It was a relief to know that Manuela had an unbreakable alibi for the time of the murder. He went topside in a cheerful frame of mind.

There were far more passengers about than there had been the day before, for the wind had dropped to Force 5, and the sea was no longer "very rough" but merely "high"—a nautical term meaning "mountainous". The unwary still tended to find themselves zigzagging on collision courses, but there was a general air of satisfaction that the worst was over.

Manuela, hollow-eyed and pale, but very beautiful, was once again embroidering her blouse, the inevitable Hadley seated by her side. Kendrick stopped, expressed his pleasure at the girl's recovery, agreed soberly that Farrell's death was a dreadful thing, and would have moved on had not Manuela patted the vacant chair and invited him to sit.

"Thanks," he said. "No risk of my getting kicked off it now."

He heard a slight gasp behind him and, turning, saw the Deck Steward gazing at him incredulously. The man's expression and what it implied were too much for Kendrick. "The Captain tells me," he said pleasantly, "that, at the time, you thought I was joking." Speechless, the steward walked on. Kendrick sat down, and found Hadley looking at him with interest.

"Well, now!" said the Englishman. "I was on the point of remarking that Rumour was a lying jade, but you've set me wondering if there was some faint foundation for it, after all."

"Foundation for what?"

"The . . . what's that beautiful U.S. Navy word, old boy? Like shuttlecock, only not."

"Scuttlebutt?"

"That's it. The scuttlebutt was that you'd cleaned Farrell out at poker, that he'd subsequently accused you of cheating, and that in the resultant argument you'd slung him into the drink; following which the skipper had slung you into the clink, to await a police escort at Greenock."

Kendrick smiled and said, "I'm afraid the truth's much less exciting. The Captain did ask me a few questions about Farrell, because it seems I was one of the last people to see the poor devil on board, but I doubt if anyone seriously thinks his death was other than an accident. My guess is that he leant over the rail to be sick, and lost his balance when she rolled."

"Sounds highly probable, old boy," Hadley agreed. "I remember once in my carefree youth, when I was sailing as Sparks in the old *Clan MacKinnon* . . ." He broke off as the ship's P.A. system crackled its preliminary warning of a broadcast.

"Attention, please," it said. "Will Mr. Donald Kendrick, of Room M20, go to the Purser's Bureau on the Main Deck. There is a radio-telephone call for him. Mr. Donald Kendrick of M20, please. Thank you."

"And that," said Kendrick, rising to his feet, "should finally scuttle the scuttlebutt. Be seeing you."

The Junior Purser on duty sent him to a glass-panelled booth in the rear of the office, and here, when he had announced himself to the unseen operator somewhere above, he was told that a Mr. Quayle was calling from London, and that they would make the connexion as soon as they were able to clear some static that was causing trouble.

Quayle was News Editor of the *Sunday Bulletin,* and Kendrick had been one of his hard-driven reporters for three years before being moved to the less exacting Features Department. He held on until the familiar voice said, "You there, Don?"

"Yeah. You got my radiogram?"

"Radiogram? No, not so far. But before you tell me about it, what's my wife's Christian name?"

Kendrick stared at the phone unbelievingly. "What did you say?" he queried.

"What's my wife's Christian name?"

"For heaven's sake, Q! If you've really forgotten it, isn't there someone around the office who might know?"

"Very funny," said Quayle, but he did not sound amused. "Do you know her name or don't you?"

"Of course I know her name, it's Deborah, but—"

"Good. I had to test you, Don, because a voice can be imitated, and I didn't want to take any chances. I mean, first we had a private enquiry agent round on Monday, trying to pump your secretary, and—"

"You had what?"

"He wanted to know all about your visit to Colombia and who you'd met there. When the girl asked why, he said he didn't know—he was merely acting for an associated agency in Montreal. Naturally we all assumed that some Colombian cuckold was—"

"Oh, naturally!" said Kendrick with heavy sarcasm.

"But then today the Webster Line told us that a man claiming to be you was aboard the *Duchess of Malfi*. As we thought you were staying in Montreal till—"

"I get it. No, I changed my plans."

"I see. Now, this radiogram you sent me. Is it about the missing passenger?"

"Oh, you know about him?"

"Agency message came in a few minutes ago. That's why I phoned. Francis X. Farrell, Canadian, feared lost overboard during gale."

"That all?"

"Yes. Is there more to it?"

"I'll say there is. Farrell—"

Static interrupted him, and he waited impatiently until the whining and screeching were tuned out and Quayle said, "Damn these atmospherics. Yes, Don?"

"Farrell was—" Again static broke in, and this time it seemed to go on even longer.

"What did you say Farrell was?" asked Quayle when the interference stopped. The screeching started again before Kendrick could even begin to reply; and at long last he got the message.

"These atmospherics," he said bitterly, when speech was

again possible, "are coming to you courtesy of the Webster Line, and are custom-made in the radio shack for each individual caller. I somehow feel you won't be receiving my telegram at all, Q, and there's no point in my trying to tell you what it contained, because they won't let me. I'll call you from Glasgow Friday—if I ever make it back to the Free World."

Angrily he hung up, and strode to the Cable and Radio section of the counter. "May I have my money back, please?" he asked.

"For the London radiogram, Mr. Kendrick? Yes, of course." The Junior Purser reached into the till. "I was just going to give it to you."

"You mean the Montreal one went through?"

"Oh yes, and a reply came down a minute ago, while you were on the phone." He handed over a telegraph form and some money.

"The London one, I take it, won't be going ever?"

The officer shook his head. "I'm afraid not," he said. "Captain's orders. And at sea, Mr. Kendrick, the Captain is God."

"He sure seems to think he is," said Kendrick bad-temperedly, and marched away. It was several seconds before he remembered the form in his hand, and halted to read it. *Farrells office says assignment bodyguard job client unnamed stop howsit widowise query Pete.*

Kendrick folded the paper, put it in his pocket, and returned to the Promenade Deck. Bill Hadley, reasonably enough, had seized the opportunity to spirit Manuela away. As a sometime radio officer in the Clan Line, he no doubt knew all the best shipboard hiding-places. The journalist sighed philosophically. Widowise, it looked as if he was fated to continue lucky at cards.

Looks were deceiving. The deals ran dead against him that night, and the best bluffing on earth cannot make three kings beat a flush in a showdown. By midnight, only sheer *expertise* had kept his shirt on his back.

If this reversal of fortune meant that he was now going to be lucky in love, that was all right with him. But if, as he suspected, it simply meant that luck had deserted him altogether . . . Ah, well! Tomorrow was another day.

THREE

There was nothing very promising about Thursday morning as seen from the cabin porthole, however. The wind had dropped still further, but grey, overcast skies were reflected in a tumbling waste of waters, and the *Duchess* was still a see-saw. She was making much better speed, though; probably not far short of her 21-knot potential. For the fifth and final time that crossing, the clock had gone forward an hour the night before; and although there was still no hint of land, there was at last the indefinable atmosphere of a voyage that is nearing its end.

Manuela was not in the restaurant for breakfast, but Kendrick's fear that she might have had a relapse was dispelled when he went up to the Promenade Deck. She was sitting in her chair, sewing something as usual, and for a miracle there was no sign of Hadley.

"Hola, hermosisimo!" he called as he approached. A Bolivian barmaid had assured him that it was Spanish for "Hi, Gorgeous!" and he only hoped she had not been kidding.

Whatever it meant, it made Manuela look up and laugh. "Some girl said that to you," she challenged.

"Certainly not," he lied. "What made you think so?"

"I know so; because *-o* is the masculine ending. To me you should have said *hermosisima*, with an *-a*. Feminine."

"Feminine is the word," Kendrick agreed, eyeing her with appreciation as he sat down beside her. "You're looking a hundred per cent again," he added, and it was almost the truth. "How do you feel?"

"Ninety per cent," she said. "After lunch perhaps it will be a hundred."

"And a hundred ten in time for the Farewell Dance tonight?"

"You are going to that?"

Kendrick looked both ways along the deck and said, "Before I decide, tell me how come your old *amigo* Bill Hadley isn't underfoot?"

Manuela's smile vanished. "Señor Hadley," she said in a tone like frostbite, "is no longer my friend, I'm afraid. He made a . . . a miscalculation last night, and when the answer wasn't what he wanted it to be, he became a little rough."

"So?"

"So now he doesn't like me. You see, Don, I am quite strong for a woman. And also I grew up with a realistic brother, who thought every girl should know how to break out of a clinch. The trick is perhaps a trifle . . . *indelicada;* but it works."

Kendrick grinned, and said, "I can imagine. Poor Señor Hadley . . . So you're not the kind of gal who needs a bodyguard?"

She regarded him appraisingly, indeed approvingly. "If I were, you would volunteer?" she asked.

"So fast it would amaze you. And now that Frank Farrell's dead . . ." He left the sentence unfinished.

Manuela looked puzzled. "I don't understand," she said.

"He was your bodyguard, wasn't he?"

"What are you talking about, Don?"

"Manuela, Frank Farrell was a private detective, and his office says he was hired to make this trip as a bodyguard. His cabin was next door to yours, and he tipped the Deck Steward to give him this chair I've inherited."

"How does that make him my bodyguard? I found out that Bill Hadley also had tipped the steward to get a chair next to mine, and he certainly didn't want to guard my body. Quite the opposite."

"There's more to it than that, honey. On Saturday I caught Farrell poking around in my cabin, and—"

"What?" The girl's amazement seemed quite genuine. "Is that true, Don?" she demanded.

"Oh yes. Later I learned that the reason he was interested in me was that I had recently been in Colombia. Now as far as I know, you're the only Colombian on board, and—"

"But I don't live there any more, Don. Two years ago, when my husband . . . died, I went to Montreal to make a new life for myself. I had friends there. My only skill is needlework— I majored in it at school—so that is how I have supported myself."

"Montreal's where Farrell lived too. But you still say you didn't hire him to make this trip?"

The girl looked at him in something near exasperation. "Of course I didn't hire him," she said. "Why should I? I've no jewels, no mink coats, no nothing. I'm a very unimportant *costurera*—sempstress, is it?—who has saved enough money to have a shoestring holiday in Europe. So whoever Farrell was guarding, it wasn't me. But probably he wasn't guarding anyone."

"His office said—"

"Perhaps his office wasn't telling the truth. Aren't private detective jobs confidential?"

"Yes, I suppose they are."

"Very well, then. And another thing—if he was guarding somebody, his death left them unprotected. Why has nothing happened to them?"

There was no answer to that, nor indeed to the suggestion that the agency might have been lying about the assignment. Kendrick was still convinced that, whether the girl knew it or not, Farrell's presence aboard had been connected in some way with hers, but there was clearly no point in pursuing the topic. "Okay, Toots, okay," he said. "And now, to change the subject, please may I monopolize you for the rest of the day, and then esquire you to the ball?"

"Even now that you know what happened to Hadley?" Her eyes were mischievous.

"It's always a challenge," said Kendrick with a grin, "to see if you can calculate better than the other guy."

By evening the only wind was of the ship's own making, the sea was smooth, the swell slow and rather pleasant. The clouds had thinned, and in places disappeared. The air was almost warm.

Kendrick and Manuela had spent a promising day together, and now, as he put on his tuxedo—reflecting that he would have to get back to calling it a dinner jacket again—he was praying for clear skies. It is a truism among sea-wolves that, even without moonlight, the last night before landfall is the best bet of the whole voyage; but that a moon—and tonight's would be the harvest moon to boot!—makes it a racing certainty.

Manuela danced, as he already knew from observation, superbly. Even in the ballroom she was the most exciting armful he had held in months, and later, up on the Sun Deck, she was doubly so. Their first kiss, like their first waltz, was a triumph of co-operative artistry and inspired improvisation. When their mouths at last disengaged he crossed his fingers and gave a pleading look at the silver goddess in the spangled sky. "In a moment of unbridled optimism," he murmured, "I told the steward to leave some champagne on ice in my cabin around now. Could I possibly talk you into having a nightcap, honey?"

Manuela looked at him for a thoughtful moment and then smiled slowly. *"Corriente!"* she said. "Consider me talked."

It was newly daylight when a knock on his cabin door woke Kendrick. He was alone, he discovered, but with the lingering fragrance of Coty's *Emeraude* on the air to prove that he had not been so for very long. Luxuriously he stretched himself and called a lazy, "Come in."

His bedroom steward appeared with pineapple juice and said, "Good morning, Mr. Kendrick. The Captain's compliments, and will you please take the earlier breakfast. He wants you to be available the moment the police come aboard."

"What time are they due, do you know?"

"Couldn't be certain, sir, but they'll probably board us at Cumbrae." He glanced out of the porthole. "We're rounding the Mull of Kintyre at the moment, so . . . say a couple of hours, or a bit over."

"Thanks," said Kendrick; filled his lungs with *Emeraude* and got out of bed.

It was good to see land through the porthole again, even better to go up and see it from the deck. The sun was rising over the distant Ayrshire coast, lighting the Arran hills far ahead to port, and the Clyde estuary was like a millpond—giving first-timers a wholly misleading impression of its habits.

Kendrick looked around him, mildly happy, and yet not nearly as happy as he ought to have been. He ought, in strict fact, to have been practically delirious; for not only had he "talked" Manuela into the previous night's felicities, he had also, during a lull in the proceedings, persuaded her to a follow-up date that evening.

The boat train from Greenock to Glasgow would arrive at St. Enoch Station, and the girl had intended to take another train thence, almost immediately, to London, where she would be met by friends. Kendrick, however, had induced her to stop overnight in Glasgow and let her friends wait one more day for the pleasure of seeing her. He had already that morning, on the way up from his cabin, instructed the Purser's Bureau to reserve rooms for them at the St. Enoch Hotel. And he had arranged with Manuela, lest they lose each other in the melee of disembarkation, to meet in the lounge there at six o'clock, for cocktails.

Why, then, wasn't he singing for sheer joy? The answer, he admitted to himself, was Captain Nicholson's message. On

Wednesday the old buzzard's suspicions had seemed something between irritating and ludicrous. But now Kendrick found himself wondering what would happen if by some wild chance the Scottish police should share them. At the best, it would certainly wash out his date with Manuela. At the worst . . .

He was so deeply sunk in gloomy speculation that he failed to see Father Maguire approaching till it was too late, and so found himself listening to a lament centring on the fact that Ireland had been invisible when they passed it in the small hours. Fortunately the monologue was brief, for the good Father was on his way up to Mass on the deck above. Kendrick, idly watching him climb the companionway, had a sudden chill feeling that he had seen this before—except that the black soutane ought to be whipping in a Force 9 wind, and the masculine ankles and feet should be hidden by Farrell's broad shoulders.

He shook himself, blinked, and looked again. It was quite ridiculous, of course. How fanciful can you get?

At 9 a.m. the *Duchess* slowed to steerage-way off the Great Cumbrae, and passengers lined the rails to watch a police launch edge alongside and two plain-clothes men jump nimbly aboard the liner. The launch sheered off again, and Kendrick made his way to the forward observation lounge, where he had been told to wait. He wondered what Nicholson might be saying to the Law; and, more important, what the Law might have to say to Donald Kendrick.

An hour later he was still wondering. It had been an hour of sheer beauty, of green and purple hills, and briefly glimpsed lochs stretching away from the Firth; but it had also been an hour of sixty long minutes, and it was a rather nettled Kendrick who was eventually summoned to the Captain's cabin and introduced by that officer to Detective-Inspector Shaw and his assistant.

"I'm sorry we had to keep you cooling your heels a wee

while," said the Inspector in no sorrowful tone, "but I don't think we'll have to detain you very much longer. Would you just tell us, Mr. Kendrick, as briefly as possible, exactly what happened on the night of Tuesday the twentythird instant, between your leaving the smokeroom and your losing consciousness?"

Kendrick had passed part of his waiting hour by mentally condensing his story to a hundred words, which he now recited. "Clear and concise," said Shaw, in a tone of admiration that could have been partly genuine. "The professional touch, aye. Now, Mr. Kendrick, I'm sure you'll recall that a great many of the lady passengers were confined to their rooms at that stage of the voyage. And maybe you won't be too surprised to learn that when the Captain here, with the assistance of the ship's Social Hostess, made a thorough check among the few ladies who had been up and about on Tuesday evening, they discovered . . . what do you think?"

What's this guy driving at? Kendrick wondered. Aloud he said, "Inspector, you go first. What do *you* think?"

Shaw looked slightly taken aback, and Kendrick thought he saw a gleam of something like sardonic pleasure in the Captain's eyes.

"I'll tell you what they discovered," the Inspector snapped. "Not one lady had troubled to put on an evening dress at all —black, white or rainbow! So the one you *say* you saw with Farrell . . ."

"Must have been shamming sick in her cabin till it was time for the rendezvous?" Kendrick offered. "By hokey, Inspector, I believe you've hit it!"

Once again Detective-Inspector Shaw had been fed the wrong cue-line, and his face showed it; but he recovered quickly. "That's it!" he said. "When the time did arrive, of course, she rose up, donned a ball-gown that would be particularly inconspicuous because nobody else was wearing one, and slipped unseen through well lit passages to her secret meet-

ing out on deck in a fifty-knot gale." He glared at the journalist. "Highly probable, isn't it?"

Kendrick had a sudden memory of Father Maguire's cas-
sock. "Put like that, it sounds ridiculous," he agreed. "But I
still swear I saw *somebody* with a black skirt."

"You're quite sure, are you," said Shaw meaningly, "that
you're not just telling us what you would *like* to have seen?"

"How's that again?"

"Mr. Kendrick," said the Inspector with spurious joviality,
"you're a journalist, and forbye you work for a very sensational
paper. Is it not the case that a straightforward 'man overboard'
accident would only get a few lines at the bottom of a page,
whereas if it could be invested with a hint of mystery and violence and sex—"

"Ah!" said Kendrick, smiling in his turn, "now I get what
you mean, Inspector. You mean I'm a goddam liar?" His lips
still smiled, but his eyes did not. "While Farrell was being accidentally swept overboard, I was being accidentally blown
against a davit or whatever, and getting wish-fulfilment halluci-
nations about glamorous decoys in evening dress. There isn't
enough proof to convict anyone of anything, so nothing happened. That it?"

Inspector Shaw looked likely to explode, but the master of
the *Duchess* abruptly became master of the situation as well.
"That's about the strength of it, Kendrick," he said with final-
ity. "I've no control, of course, over what you write in your
own newspaper, but—"

"No," said Kendrick acidly, "but my Editor has, and if it
differs materially from the official version he'll want concrete
proof to support it, which of course I don't have. Ah, well, you
can't win them all! Shall I dictate my disembowelled statement
to your sergeant, Inspector, or will you dictate it to me?"

The *Duchess* had been at anchor in mid-stream for fortyfive
minutes and the tender had taken off most of the passengers
and baggage by the time Kendrick read over a milk-and-water

series of half-truths, scowled, and signed at the bottom of the page.

"Thank you, sir, thank you," said Shaw urbanely, putting the document into his brief-case. "If you should be wanted for the Sheriff's Inquiry—that's our Scots equivalent of a coroner's inquest—you'll be notified, of course. But I think it's unlikely you'll be called."

"I," said Kendrick, "think it's quite certain that I won't. Good morning, gentlemen. And thanks for the ride, Captain." He gave the detectives a five-yard start, and was about to follow them when Nicholson tapped him restrainingly on the arm. He halted, turned.

The Captain waited until the Law had disappeared, and then said, "Kendrick, I . . . Dammit, I liked the way you handled that windbag!"

"Thank you, Captain."

Nicholson regarded him thoughtfully. "It's probably true," he said, "that nobody could ever dig up any real evidence now. And no doubt you know better than I do why these shore-side fellows don't want to waste their energies trying. I gave you a kind of a rough time on Wednesday, but . . ." He paused, stared Kendrick straight in the eyes, and held out his hand. "Willing to shake?" he asked.

Kendrick looked at him, liked him, and grinned. "Eager," he said, and shook the hard brown hand warmly.

"Mind you," said the Captain judicially, "I don't approve of *anyone* getting away with murder. But if somebody has to in this case—well, lad, I'm glad it's you!"

Kendrick missed the boat train and, while waiting for the supplementary service, put through a phone-call to Quayle. The News Editor was, if anything, even more disgusted than he, but agreed that the *Bulletin* would be going right out on a limb if it printed Kendrick's story.

"We've been accused too often lately of tarting up the facts to boost our sales," he said with regret, "so we daren't risk it again. There's a faint smell of high level hush-up about this anyway. It's a pity, Don, but never mind. Just try to forget the whole fiasco and enjoy what's left of your leave."

"That's exactly what I'm going to do," said Kendrick, the pleasing image of Manuela coming into his mind. "Starting this very night!"

Somewhere, no doubt, his Bad Fairy was having a malicious little laugh at that one.

FOUR

At five minutes to six Kendrick walked into the St. Enoch Hotel lounge and told the waiter he would not order anything until his guest arrived. Twenty minutes later he changed his mind and called for a dry Martini. At six-thirty he went to the reception desk and asked for the number of Manuela's room. The clerk consulted the book and said, "There's no Mrs. Gomez registered, sir."

Kendrick frowned. "She hasn't arrived yet, you mean?" he said. "I know she has a reservation. It was made from shipboard this morning."

"From the *Duchess of Malfi,* sir?"

"Yep."

The clerk reached out for a typewritten list. "We have quite a number of *Duchess* passengers here tonight," he said as he ran his eye down it. "Yes, here we are. Mrs. Gomez. But she's cancelled it."

"Cancelled it? You're sure?"

"Well, somebody has, sir. I don't know who, or when, because I only came on duty half an hour ago, but it's marked here as having been cancelled by phone."

"I see," said the journalist, trying not to look tight-lipped. "Are there any messages for me? Kendrick, 409."

The man glanced at a nest of pigeonholes behind him, shook his head. "I'm afraid not, sir," he said.

"Thank you. I just discovered that I have to catch a night train south and won't be staying here after all, but of course I'll pay for my room. I'm going up to pack now, and after that

I'll be in the dining-room. Could you send my bill to me in there?"

"Certainly, sir. I'm sorry you've had to change your plans."

"Believe me," said Kendrick sincerely, "you're not half as sorry as I am."

He turned towards the elevators, then halted abruptly. Bill Hadley was standing a few feet away, regarding him with an amused smile. "Well, well!" said the Englishman. "First we were in the same ship, now apparently we're in the same boat."

"Meaning?" said Kendrick.

Hadley shrugged. "Meaning, old boy," he said, "that the lady turned me down, and now she's stood you up. Why don't we get together and drown each other's sorrows?"

"Thanks," said Kendrick, "but I've a train to catch, and I want to pack and eat first."

"Ah, come on, old boy. At least you have time for a swift snort." He laid a hand on the Canadian's arm.

"I really don't, I'm afraid," said Kendrick, freeing himself and walking on. He was darned if he was going to spend the evening discussing feminine fickleness with a man who called him "old boy" every few seconds. But he was even more darned if he could understand why Manuela had agreed to the date at all, if she had intended to walk out on it.

A lift reached ground level and disgorged a middle-aged couple who had been aboard the *Duchess*. They smiled at him, and his smarting soul read pity into it. On the fourth floor, as he walked along to his room, he met yet another ex-passenger, who gave him a wink and a cheerful, "Ay, ay, Don? No winsome widow tonight?" Obviously, the sooner he was out of this place, the better. Luckily he had very little packing to do.

He opened the bedroom door, switched on the lights, and stopped in dismay. There was more packing to do than he had bargained for. Two of his three suitcases had been opened, and their contents lay scattered all over the floor. The third had been unstrapped but not unlocked, though the same key would have opened all three. Presumably the intruder had not had time.

And that meant that the intruder had been tipped off that Kendrick was on his way up, sooner than expected. The intruder must have had a colleague downstairs keeping watch, and that colleague had telephoned the bedroom when the journalist headed for the lift. The look-out could have been anyone at all, of course, but he wondered if it was mere coincidence that Mr. William "Old Boy" Hadley had tried so hard to delay his return to the room.

He had almost finished packing when the phone rang and the switchboard operator said she had a personal call for him. The caller was Manuela.

"Where the heck are you, honey?" he asked.

"I . . . Don, I . . . Something unexpected came up, and I had to change my plans. I'm terribly sorry to break our appointment."

"Where and when can we have another?"

"Oh, as soon as ever I . . . Don, where do you live in London?"

"Six-o-seven Castlemaine Court, Chelsea," said Kendrick promptly, and gave her his phone number. "But aren't—"

"Please, I have very little time. When will you get home?"

"Tomorrow morning. I'm heading south in an hour or two."

"Then tomorrow—" She broke off, and Kendrick heard the murmur of a man's voice in the background. It stopped, and Manuela said, "I don't know quite when I'll be heading south, Don, but tomorrow I'll either call you from—from wherever I am, or send you a message. Goodnight, *amor mio.*" Click.

Kendrick depressed the cradle-bar, then released it. The hotel switchboard came on, and he said, "That personal call for me just now—d'you happen to know whether it was local or long distance?"

"Long distance, Mr. Kendrick," said the operator immedi-

ately. "The exchange spoke to me first. It was . . . oh, somewhere in the north of England . . . Yes. Doncaster."

"Thanks a lot," said Kendrick, and hung up. Doncaster, he
estimated, must be well over two hundred miles from Glasgow.
For a girl who didn't know when she would be heading south,
Manuela seemed to have covered a fair distance in that direction in a pretty short space of time.

Later he stretched out in his berth in the train and thought
about her. What he thought was that she had almost certainly
been lying when she denied any knowledge of Farrell's assignment. The detective had to have been guarding her, and now,
bereft of him, she had been forced into hiding. That much
seemed obvious. And equally obvious was the fact that, whatever she might be, it was certainly more than "a very unimportant *costurera*". The Case of the Secretive Sempstress, Perry
Mason might have called it. Or maybe not.

His eyes closed, and he remembered that he had had little
sleep the previous night. Not that he was complaining about
that. Indeed, another wakeful night on the same terms would
have been most acceptable. Still, hadn't happened. Doncaster,
for Pete's sake! Goodnight, *amor mio*. 'Night, honey.

After a time he dreamed. He dreamed that it was Hallowe-
e'en, and that for his sins he was spending it Canadian style,
with fireworks, and with his three small nephews. The little
pests had dared him to light a giant firecracker and hold it till
it exploded, and like a fool he had accepted the challenge. The
fuze burned down and then came the bang, so loud and real
that it woke him. He was briefly aware of a figure standing over
him, and then something soft and damp was pressed firmly on
his face, and he smelt ether.

Reflex action rather than will sent his head jerking side-
ways, and he heard a thud on the pillow by his ear. One arm,
by a happy chance, was outside the bedclothes, so he grabbed
the wrist above the ether pad and twisted viciously. The
man lost his balance, and the second blackjack blow cracked

against woodwork. Then Kendrick's other hand was free, and he had a wrist in each of them.

The dim blue night-light showed him only a medium-sized form with no discernible face, but he could hear heavy breathing as the man strove to break his grip. Blackjack and cotton-wool fell to the floor; and then slowly, as Kendrick increased his pressure, the attacker was forced to his knees.

The journalist was sitting up now, methodically pushing and pulling his feet clear of the sheets. He heard his opponent take a deep breath, as for a supreme effort, and tightened his grip yet further. The man gave a convulsive jerk that brought him halfway to his feet, then slumped limply to the floor.

Suspecting a trick, Kendrick retained his grasp of both wrists as he swung his legs out of bed. But there was no sign of movement from his opponent, and after a time he risked dropping one wrist and snatching up the fallen blackjack. Then he dropped the other wrist and, without taking his eyes off target, reached out and switched on the lights.

The fellow wore a brown pin-stripe suit, suede shoes and gloves, a yellow button-down shirt and a polka-dotted bow tie. He also wore a nylon stocking over his head. Kendrick pulled it off, to disclose open, sightless eyes and a face so twisted that it was some seconds before he recognized it. It was the face of the man he had known as Father Maguire, and two things seemed fairly clear; the first, that the role of priest had been strictly masquerade; the second, that he was dead.

Kendrick opened the window to sling out the ether pad, and fog rolled in. Since waking, he had been subconsciously aware that the train was running slowly, and now he understood why. He understood, too, the sound that had wakened him. This coach was immediately behind the locomotive, and the bang must have been the detonation of a fog-signal fastened to the rail. He closed the window again and wondered what the devil to do.

There was no question, of course, about his legal duty. He

ought to call the guard of the train and tell him the full story of the struggle. And maybe that would be not only legal, but smart too. Maybe, again, it wouldn't. Maybe some cop more conscientious than Inspector Shaw might think it odd that Donald Kendrick was always Johnny-on-the-spot when a *Duchess of Malfi* passenger met sudden death.

He wished he knew what had killed Maguire. A heart attack seemed likely, but just how blameless are you if someone has a heart attack while you're practically breaking both his arms? Kendrick's knowledge of law was sketchy, but he did know that in Britain a plea of self-defence stands or falls on the degree of force used, and that no more may be used than the minimum necessary to ensure the user's safety. He had an unpleasant feeling that the marks on Maguire's wrists were not consistent with such moderation—the more so as the man had dropped his weapon and the ether pad long before he died.

Kendrick looked at his watch. It was just after two o'clock —about five hours to go till London, if the train was on time, which seemed unlikely. He opened the window again and peered out, but could see nothing. He closed it and started to dress. Whatever course he might decide to follow, he would feel better with his clothes on.

By the time he was knotting his shoelaces he had made up his mind. The fog had been his friend once—but for that fog-signal Maguire would have put him out without waking him —and it could be his friend again. With the engine-crew peering ahead, the guard a dozen fog-shrouded coaches away to the rear, and all right-thinking passengers wrapped in slumber, it was millions to one against anyone's seeing a body fall from the train.

The compartment window, unfortunately, looked too small for a disposal-hatch, and he did not want to risk wedging the body half in and half out of it. The windows in the coach doors, however, would be ample-sized, and the chances of meeting anyone in the corridor at this hour were negligible.

He opened his door and looked out. Nobody. He switched off the main compartment light and, in the blue gloom, hoisted Maguire to his feet.

The obvious way to carry him was in a fireman's hold, but Kendrick hesitated. One never knew. And in the remote event of his being seen in the well lit corridor the fireman's carry would register vividly. It would be less noteworthy, if also less convenient, to drag the corpse.

He looped one dead arm round his neck and held its wrist, then put his own arm round Maguire's waist, hooked the door open with his foot, and set off on his ten-yard trip. Before he had taken three paces the remote event occurred. A compartment door opened, and a grey-haired lady in a dressing-gown was looking at him from a range of about two feet.

Secure in the knowledge that Maguire's lolling head kept his tell-tale face from showing, Kendrick lurched and said, "Fella'sh drunk. Jush can't hold it." The lady took a swift step backwards and slammed her door. Sweating slightly, the journalist resumed his gruesome journey.

Once round the corner in the tiny vestibule he breathed more freely. He propped Maguire against the wall, jamming him there with his shoulder while he lowered the window as far as it would go. Outside, the fog seemed thicker than ever. Then his eye caught the familiar little notice, *It is dangerous to lean out of the window,* and he smiled without mirth. "Don't worry, Paddy," he murmured. "That doesn't mean you. Not any more."

He pushed Maguire's head and chest through the opening and let them hang over. Then he stooped, grasped both ankles, and heaved. The thud as the body landed was surprisingly faint.

Seconds later he heard brakes go into action, and the train clanked to a stop. There was complete and utter silence.

For a moment of near panic Kendrick thought someone had seen him and pulled the alarm chain. Then he realised that, with all this fog about, it was more likely that the train had a signal against it. He looked out of the window, saw the faint fuzzy glow of a red light ahead, and breathed again. Yes, a signalman had stopped them. But what a heck of a time to choose, with Maguire's body lying in potential view of some rearward coach window; perhaps the guard's.

He thought of returning to his compartment, remembered the grey-haired lady, and changed his mind. She had almost certainly been going along to the toilet, and would doubtless reappear for that purpose at the precise moment that he passed her door again—without Maguire. No, it wasn't worth risking. He went through the connecting porch to the next coach and swiftly strode to its far end. He noticed with interest that he was walking on tiptoe.

He locked himself in the toilet, looked at his watch, and decided to emerge in fifteen minutes. It was the longest quarter-hour of his life.

The train jerked into motion again a minute after six, and was running rather than crawling by the time he regained his compartment. A further fifteen minutes saw it return to somewhere not far short of normal speed, and he wondered if he had dumped Maguire just inside the fog-belt. From the feel of things, he had, and was now being borne away from the scene of the crime at a reassuring rate. He relaxed, undressed again, and then threw blackjack and stocking out of the window.

A moment later his mind started to function fully, and he wished he had kept the blackjack. He could not imagine what the pseudo-priest had been up to, but the discovery that he was pseudo pointed clearly to one conclusion: that it had indeed been Maguire who decoyed Frank Farrell to his death. And that had been no single-handed murder. At least one other person had been involved—the strong-arm sentry who had knocked out Kendrick. Suppose he too was aboard the train? And suppose, when Maguire failed to return from his mission . . .

Kendrick looked doubtfully at the flimsy bolt on the compartment door, and guessed that one decent shove from outside would dislodge it. He sighed, and started to put on his clothes again. He had better have another wakeful night after all.

FIVE

In the event, the precaution proved needless. The rest of the run was normal, and the train pulled in less than half an hour behind time.

London was sunny and appreciably warmer than Scotland had been, and Kendrick kept the cab windows open as he was driven from Euston Station to Chelsea. He smiled with affection at familiar landmarks, at the big red double-decker buses, at the sight of an unarmed policeman, at the pubs in which one could buy real draught English bitter. It was good to be back—and even better to be back with a week's leave still to run, and the prospect of meeting Manuela Gomez during it.

As he alighted at Castlemaine Court the hall porter hurried out with a welcoming smile, helped him with his luggage, and told him it was a pleasure to see him again.

"Thanks, Howard," said Kendrick. "Did the manager get my cable from Quebec?"

"He did, sir. The flat's been cleaned and the fridge stocked up as per."

"Good show," said Kendrick, dropping right back into the English idiom as if he had never been away. "Don't bother coming up in the lift, Howard, I can manage these bags myself."

His little furnished apartment on the top floor had been cleaned, all right, and the parquet flooring polished within an inch of its life. After days of walking on wet, unstable decks, he reflected, it would be ironic if he slipped and broke a leg in his own bedroom.

Ten minutes later, tubbed and shaved, he was about to

scramble some eggs when the house phone buzzed. It was Howard. "There's a gentleman down here would like to see you, Mr. Kendrick," he said. "I've told him you're only just back, but—"

"Who is he?"

"A Mr. Gomez, sir," said the porter, and Kendrick's stomach gave a slight heave. "Would you like to speak to him?"

"No," said the journalist, "but I suppose I'd better. Put him on, will you?"

A suave voice with the barest trace of an accent said, "Mr. Kendrick, a thousand apologies for intruding on you at this hour, but I'm afraid my business is urgent. It concerns your recent transatlantic voyage, as you've probably guessed. It need not take five minutes of your time, but I'd be most grateful if you'd give me the five minutes right away."

"Okay," said Kendrick without enthusiasm. "Come on up."

And what, he wondered, was this? Some kind of blackmail project? A challenge to a duel? Or what? If Manuela wasn't really a widow . . . He had a sudden memory of their talk on Thursday morning, when she had explained how she came to be living in Canada. "Two years ago, when my husband . . . died," she had said, with an appreciable hesitation before the verb. If the guy wasn't dead at all, and was now on his way upstairs, then the five minutes might be quite unpleasant. He shook his head sadly. These things simply shouldn't happen, and certainly not before breakfast.

The visitor proved to be a solid, well dressed fellow of about forty, with olive skin and a thin line of moustache. He accepted a chair, declined coffee, and said, "Mr. Kendrick, you and my wife were fellow-passengers in the *Duchess of Malfi* this week."

"That," said the journalist, "makes you the most substantial ghost I ever met."

The man smiled slightly. "I am no ghost," he admitted, "but if the Colombian authorities knew I was still alive I might soon become one. You possibly know, Mr. Kendrick, that there was an unsuccessful attempt some time back to revise the system of government in my country."

"I was under the impression," said Kendrick, "that there was an attempt every month or so."

The Colombian frowned. "I am not referring," he said coldly, "to the terrorist activities of Communist hoodlums, but to the uprising of the *norteños* two years ago under Colonel Carlos Urquiza." He spoke the name like a fanfare.

Kendrick nodded. "I remember," he said. "They wanted home rule for the north, or something. But it rather misfired, didn't it?"

"Unfortunately, that is so. When it failed, I was one of those able to evade arrest and leave the country. Moreover I had the good fortune to do it in circumstances which made it seem certain that I had been drowned while trying to make Jamaica by sailboat. I accepted the luck gratefully, and stayed dead. Manuela too had to leave, and went to live with friends in Canada. When I reached England and safety, of course, I got in touch with her. And now at last she has been able to make this journey to be reunited with me."

If that's the truth, said Kendrick to himself, *she sure took a fond farewell of her Merry Widowhood.* Aloud he said, "And have you been reunited?"

A cloud crossed the other's face. "By telephone only," he said. "Something has arisen which makes it imprudent for us to meet until . . . well, for some days to come. And that brings me to the point of my visit. I want the papers that she gave you to take ashore for her, in case she was searched at the *aduana* —the Customs."

Kendrick looked at him non-committally. "What makes you think she gave me some papers?" he asked.

"She told me so on the phone last night. She said that Farrell had been washed overboard, but she had found someone else to bring the papers ashore—you. She was carrying these papers to me, Mr. Kendrick, and it's vitally important that I have them immediately. Please hand them over."

Kendrick smiled and shook his head. "You may or may not be her husband," he said, "but you're certainly a liar, and your bluff hasn't come off. Manuela gave me nothing to take ashore for her."

Suddenly the visitor was on his feet with a gun in his hand, a slim little revolver that might not be very dangerous at long range but could no doubt be quietly lethal in a small room. "I want these papers, Kendrick," he said softly. "Will you give them to me, or must I kill you and then search your apartment for them?"

"You think you'd get away with it?"

The Colombian smiled thinly. "I don't use my real name in England," he said. "When I walk out of this building Mr. Gomez will cease to exist and I shall disappear into my other identity—which has nothing whatever to connect it with Manuela or the late Mr. Kendrick."

The journalist eyed him thoughtfully, then said, "You win, I guess. If I tell you where the papers are, do you promise—"

"You don't tell me where they are, my friend, you get them for me; while I keep this little gun on you to ensure that you try no tricks."

Kendrick shrugged and rose to his feet, watched warily by Gomez. "I didn't know who the heck you might be when we spoke on the phone," he said, crossing the room. "So I slipped them out of sight the first place that was handy." He stepped onto the parquet surround, bent down, groped under the edge of the big Bokhara rug, and then tugged it violently. It whipped out from under the gunman's feet and sent him flying.

The revolver cracked, and the sound of a bullet smacking into woodwork preceded the crash as Gomez hit the floor. Kendrick dived on top of him with a knee on his gun-wrist, and chopped hard on the man's neck with the edge of his hand. The visitor went limp.

Kendrick dropped the gun into his bathrobe pocket and proceeded to glance through the South American's wallet. There was a goodly amount of money, a set of postcards that outplayed *Playboy*, and an international driving-licence issued in Havana to one Primo Alberdi.

In the kitchen the house phone buzzed, and he went through to answer it. It was Howard the hall porter again. "Are you all right, sir?" he asked.

"I'm fine, thanks. Why?"

"It's Mrs. Forrest in 507, sir. She rang down to say she'd heard a terrific bump, and she thought you might have fallen and hurt yourself."

"Ah," said Kendrick, "yes. It must have shaken her ceiling quite a bit." His mind was racing. If he told the porter the truth there would be a squad car round within minutes; and he did not want the police to arrive until he had questioned Señor Alberdi in some detail. Come to think of it, after his own exploit on the night train, the less police attention he drew to himself the better. "The bump wasn't me," he said, "it was Mr. Gomez. He doesn't seem to have suffered any serious damage, but that's not the cleaner's fault. Where did she learn to polish floors, Howard? At a curling rink?"

"Made it a little slippy, has she, sir?"

"Understatement of the year."

"I'll mention it to her, Mr. Kendrick."

"Do that, will you? And please thank Mrs. Forrest for telling you so promptly." He hung up, stepped into the little lobby, and found the outside door ajar. Primo Alberdi, he discovered, was no longer in the lounge.

Kendrick muttered an ornate oath and wondered what to do. With nothing on but a bathrobe and slippers he could hardly chase the man, and if he phoned and asked Howard to stop him, in would come the Law. The only other course was to let him escape. Sadly, he closed the door.

After checking the flat thoroughly to make sure that Alberdi really had left, and was not hiding somewhere with intent to resume the argument when his opponent was off guard, Kendrick went more methodically through the man's wallet. Apart from the phone numbers of Pam, Beryl and Lisette, however, and a membership card for the Philoptic Club—*Bring your own glasses, we provide the spectacles!*—it contained little that he had not already seen. Specifically and annoyingly, it contained no clue to Alberdi's occupation or address.

While he cooked and ate breakfast he pondered on the mysterious "papers" that Manuela was supposed to have given him. Was that what Maguire had come to his compartment seeking, what Maguire or somebody else had earlier been looking for in his room at the St. Enoch? Alberdi obviously believed in their existence, and was quite sure that Kendrick had them, so . . . An unpleasant notion occurred to him. Was it possible that he did have them all the time? Could Manuela have slipped something into his baggage in his cabin while he slept, intending to recover it as soon as he fell asleep again in the Glasgow hotel?

It was a deflating explanation of her sweet surrender on Thursday night and her implied willingness to repeat the frolic on Friday, but he ruefully admitted to himself that it might well be true. If Farrell's death had in fact robbed her of not only a bodyguard but also a courier, and if she really feared the Customs search so much, then maybe Maguire had made a very intelligent guess. And passed it on to Alberdi? The Irishman could have seen Kendrick and Manuela together a dozen times on Thursday, might even—for he had admitted being up and about in the early hours of Friday, ostensibly hoping for a glimpse of Ireland—have seen the girl leaving Kendrick's cabin or regaining her own. So, if he really believed she was seeking a replacement for Farrell, the journalist was obviously it.

Carefully he unpacked his three cases, shaking out each garment in turn before putting it away, probing every pocket, even unfolding his handkerchiefs and feeling in the toes of shoes and socks. Not a thing. Papers there were a-plenty, but they were all his own, and he checked them sheet by sheet to prove it. There was nothing hidden in his typewriter case either. Whatever dangerous documents Manuela might have been carrying, she had apparently risked taking them ashore in person. The conclusion helped his ego to recover somewhat.

As he was dressing—for the third time that morning—a button came off his sports jacket, and he looked at it sadly. This was where Manuela would have been useful, he thought, for when it came to needle and thread he was a Grade A stumblethumb, whereas she . . . by hokey! Was it possible after all?

He took his dinner jacket from the wardrobe and looked at its inside. It had to be this or nothing, he felt, for it was the only silk-lined garment he possessed, and therefore the only one that would rustle whether it had papers sewn into it or not.

The stitching certainly looked professional, but then Manuela was. He tested the cloth between thumb and finger, but felt nothing unusual. The only way was to open it up. With his penknife he carefully unpicked six inches or so along the bottom edge of the lining, inserted his hand and groped around. Pay dirt! Gently he extracted a very flat envelope made of India paper, some seven or eight inches long by five across. It was sealed but unaddressed.

So this was the secret of his success! He felt flatter than the envelope. Kendrick the Great Lover had turned out to be Donald the Dupe, private carrier pigeon. There he had lain, a sleeping sucker, while the recent partner of his joys got down to the real purpose of her visit.

It had been no spur-of-the-moment idea either, for she must have had the envelope and sewing materials in her handbag all evening. What a girl! She had played it perfectly; knowing he would invite her to his cabin, guessing with dead accuracy that he would later suggest a date ashore, and letting him, not too easily, persuade her to agree. Talk about double-dealing! It was enough to put a man off women for life.

His personal reaction, however, soon faded before his professional one. Chance had dealt him into a mystery story, and now here in his hand, almost certainly, lay the key to it. After only the briefest hesitation he slit open the envelope and pulled out half-a-dozen wafer-thin sheets covered with tiny block capitals in six-letter groups. Clearly it was a cipher of some kind, and until he could get a cryptographer to work on it he would not know the nature of his prize, though he had no doubts of its value. Maguire and Alberdi hadn't been playing any penny-ante game. This was going to be News.

The best cryptographer he knew was the *Bulletin*'s chess correspondent, a Brighton schoolmaster who had been an Admiralty code-breaker during the war. But old Markham was a small-boat maniac and spent all his weekends afloat, so he would not be available till Monday. And this was only Saturday, and plenty could happen between now and then. The papers must be put out of the enemy's reach for the weekend, and what safer place could one ask than Her Majesty's mails? He sealed the little sheaf in a manila envelope, addressed it to himself c/o Poste Restante at the Sloane Square post office, donned a jacket with its full quota of buttons, and went out. When he had dropped the envelope into the nearest mailbox he felt considerably easier of mind.

He walked on down King's Road in the sunshine, enjoying the unfamiliar Saturday atmosphere; thought happily of his colleagues hard at work compiling the morrow's *Bulletin;* and mentally foretasted his first pint of bitter in nearly three months. Then he heard someone calling his name and, turning, saw a small but pleasingly shaped figure in a sweater and pants hurrying after him. Her red hair swung casually free, horn-rimmed glasses sat attractively astride her tip-tilted nose, and there was more than a hint of the pixie about her pointed little chin.

"Well!" he said. "Talk about perfect timing! I was just thinking of you, Lynn, believe it or not."

Lynn Everett grinned and said, "Not. But what are you doing here anyway? I thought you were still chasing glamorous señoritas round moonlit patios."

"Got back this morning," said Kendrick, smiling down at her affectionately and completely forgetting that he had just gone off women for life. She was a good foot shorter than himself, weighed ninety-five pounds, and was guessed by most people to be about eighteen—until she grinned, when they promptly subtracted three years. In fact she was twentyfour, and worked in Foreign Office Security.

It occurred to him that, with her contacts, she might have some inside dope on current Colombian matters, so he said, "They'll be open in a few minutes. Join me in a quiet quencher."

"I wish I could, but I've got to get home and make lunch for some friends who're coming round."

"How long will they be staying?"

Lynn's green eyes lit up. "Have you some personal reason for wanting to know?" she asked hopefully.

"Well," said Kendrick, "if you're going to be free by the evening, perhaps we might have a bite of food together. You know, like sandwiches in the launderette while I deal with my travel-stained lingerie."

"It sounds enchanting. May I bring a few sheets and pillow-cases?"

"Sure. The more the merrier, and we'll make a night of it. Seven o'clock suit?"

Lynn said that seven would be fine, and they parted. Kendrick resumed his stroll, and in the fullness of time found that a pint of bitter from the wood was quite as exquisite as his memory of it.

He lunched in a café and then went to the public library, where he obtained a number of newspaper files. The Colombian rising of two years back might or might not have some connexion with this present business, but there was no harm in brushing up on his knowledge of it.

His vague recollections proved correct. Colonel Urquiza and his devoted *norteños* (which seemed simply to mean "northerners") had sought to gain autonomy for the Departments of Magdalena and Norte de Santander, but had evidently underestimated the size of their task, for the movement had ended in a couple of weeks and a few executions. Urquiza himself had escaped, allegedly with foreign assistance, and was believed to be living quietly in Spain now, under another name.

Outside the library Kendrick bought an early *Evening Post* and found that "Fog Blankets North" was so far the main story of the day. The item he sought had just made the Late News column. *Unidentified man found dead on railway line near Carnforth (Lancs). Believed fallen from train.* Unidentified, huh? Perhaps that was not altogether surprising.

From Chelsea a bus took him to Shaftesbury Avenue, and he walked from there to Old Compton Street, where Alberdi's Philoptic Club was situated. The club was closed, but a showcase full of photographs left no room for doubt as to the nature of the spectacles it would provide when it opened. *Club hours 8 p.m. to 2 a.m., Sats. 7 p.m. to 11.30 p.m.* said a notice. *Members only. E. J. Buchanan, Manager.* His investigations temporarily halted, Kendrick went home.

As he entered his flat he stopped short, sniffing. Tobacco— but he himself was a non-smoker. Furthermore the lounge door was ajar, though he was certain he had closed it before he went out. As he looked at it, he heard the slight creak of a chair inside the room.

Swiftly he stepped into the bathroom, where his robe hung behind the door. Whoever the intruder might be, Alberdi's pistol would not come amiss. He felt in both pockets of the robe, swore softly. The little gun was gone.

SIX

Kendrick returned to the hall to find his visitor standing in the lounge doorway—a tall, athletic figure in the middle fifties, with fair hair, a healthy outdoor tan, and well cut tweeds. There was nothing more deadly in his hand than a cheroot.

"Good afternoon, Kendrick," he said. He had a pleasant, almost accentless English voice. "When you didn't come into the lounge I thought you might have spotted me and gone straight to the phone, but I'm glad I was wrong."

"Just who the blazes may you be?" said Kendrick.

"Doe is the name," said the stranger. "John Doe. I hope you'll forgive my making free with your flat, but I was afraid that if I waited downstairs a porter might appear and ask my business."

"You found my door unlocked, of course."

John Doe smiled slightly. "After a few seconds, yes," he agreed. "I happened to have some skeleton keys with me. Kendrick, could we sit down and talk for a minute? I'm here with a message from Manuela Gomez about that envelope."

"It's a popular role," said Kendrick, following him into the lounge.

The older man looked at him sharply. "What exactly do you mean?" he asked.

"You're the second messenger I've had today. The first went even farther than you, though—he said he was the late Mr. Gomez. Report of his death greatly exaggerated."

"Manuela's husband was a chap called Ramon Belgrano. She resumed her maiden name when she went to Canada."

"She really is a widow, then?"

"Most certainly. She was widowed by a firing squad after the Urquiza rising; and spent a pretty grim month in jail herself while they debated whether to shoot her too, or merely kick her out of the country." He saw Kendrick's incredulous expression, and grinned. "Oh, yes," he said, "Manuela took a very active part in that revolt, believe it or not. I'm sure you have found her quite delightful, Kendrick, but her nickname in certain Colombian circles is *La Cascabela,* which isn't as pretty as it sounds. It's South American Spanish for the female rattlesnake. But about this chap who said he was her husband. Have—"

"I think his name's Primo Alberdi. Do you know him?"

"Not from Adam. But I'm glad you didn't give him the letter."

"What makes you think I didn't?"

"My dear fellow! I saw his wallet in your bedroom. When a man leaves his wallet and—I suspect, because it's a Cuban *Cabrito*—his gun in a stranger's flat, it suggests that he didn't depart on top of the situation."

Kendrick nodded agreement with this reasoning, and said, "How do I know you're not another phoney, Mr.—uh—Doe?"

The visitor smiled faintly. "Believe me," he said, "I've a good reason for withholding my name. As to proving my *bona fides,* I asked Manuela to give me a note of introduction to you, but she said you had never seen her handwriting, and wouldn't know whether it was genuine; so the best I can do is tell you that I was beside her when she made that personal phone-call to you at the St. Enoch. Would you like me to repeat her end of the conversation?"

"Just tell me where she called from."

"A petrol station on the outskirts of Doncaster," said the other without hesitation. "We stopped on our way south."

"And where is she now?"

This time John Doe did hesitate. "I'm afraid I can't tell you," he said at last. "The message she sent was a sincere apology for having tricked you, and a request that you give me the letter."

"It's not here."

"I'd already come to that conclusion. But you know where it is, because you discovered it in the lining of your dinner jacket. If you hadn't, I'd have collected it and been away from here hours ago. That was Plan A. Plan B, if I found I couldn't get into the flat while you were out of it, was to tell you where the thing was hidden, and deliver Manuela's message. Neither of us foresaw that you might come on it for yourself. Where is it now, Kendrick?"

"Temporarily out of my possession," said Kendrick truthfully. "It will be quite safe till I decide on the best way of using it."

"But dammit, man, it's not yours."

"That," said the journalist, "is a point I'm prepared to go into with Manuela, but with nobody else. As I understand the law, she gave up her title to the letter when she parted from it. If she'd commissioned me to take it ashore for her, of course, it would have been a different matter. Why didn't she anyway?"

John Doe shrugged. "Exactly what I asked her myself," he said. "She says she didn't want to have to make a long series of explanations, and also she was afraid that if you knew you had it you'd look guilty or nervous, and the Customs fellows would become suspicious. As you're probably aware, they can compel you to open any sealed package if they feel like it, and . . . well, rightly or wrongly, Manuela thought it was safer to do what she did."

"That's just too bad," said Kendrick. "If she'd trusted me, all this would never have happened; and, of course, I'd never have got the story I'm quite sure I'll find in that letter when I have it decoded."

"Story!" said John Doe bitterly. "Kendrick, there's battle, murder and sudden death in that letter—and Manuela had to plant it on a bloody journalist!" He sighed, then recovered himself. "I'll be in touch again when I've had a chance to talk to the girl," he said, heading for the door. "Maybe she'll have some suggestion for getting you to co-operate. I'm beaten—unless you're bribable?"

"Of course I'm bribable. Who isn't?"

John Doe stopped short in the little hall. "How much?" he asked curtly. "For the letter undecoded."

"What do you offer?"

"Five thousand?"

"Words? Or merely pounds?"

The visitor smiled grimly. "I was pretty sure you weren't," he said, and opened the front door. "I haven't pinched that *Cabrito,* by the way. It's under a cushion on the couch, and the ammo's in the little drawer in your desk, beside your business cards." He went out.

Kendrick closed the door, streaked for the house phone and buzzed the hall porter. "Call the first cab on the rank, Howard," he said. "You know all the drivers, don't you?"

"Yes, sir."

"Tell him to try and look as if he'd just dropped a fare. There's a man on his way downstairs." He described John Doe. "He may or may not hire the cab—he may be suspicious, or have his own car, or take a bus or something—but in any case there's a quid or two in it for the cabbie if he can tell me where the chap goes. Can fix?"

"Can try, sir," said Howard, and hung up.

Kendrick relaxed, and pondered on what he had learned from his visitor. So Manuela had been married to Ramon Belgrano, had she? The name had appeared almost as often as Colonel Urquiza's in the press reports he had read at the library, for Belgrano had been the Colonel's right-hand man. And Manuela herself had been active enough in the revolt to come near execution, and to acquire the uncompromising sobriquet of Rattlesnake! Well, well! As John Doe had said,

La Cascabela sounded much prettier. But it's the thought that counts.

He heard the house phone buzz in the kitchen, and hurried to answer it.

"Worked a treat, sir," Howard announced. "Alf Groves was first on the rank, and he's a bright kid. Got the idea right away. He put on a bit of an act, and the gent did hire him. Told him Paddington Station, but Alf'll be reporting to you himself when he gets back."

"Thanks, Howard," said Kendrick. "Send him right up when he comes, will you?"

He showered and dressed for his dinner-date, and had just completed the operation when a thin-faced young man arrived and introduced himself as Alf Groves. "Fare changed his mind about Paddington, sir," he said with obvious satisfaction.

"He did?"

"Yes, sir. First off, though, I didn't think he was going to hire me at all. I was searching in the back when he come out, and he asked me if someone had lost something, so I said my last fare thought she might have dropped an ear-ring. He said, 'Funny she didn't wait to see if you found it'—sounding a bit suspicious-like, if you get me—so I said, 'Well, the way her little boy was hopping and twisting, she probably thought it was more important to get him to the bathroom in time.' Then I sung out to Bert Howard, 'You can tell her it ain't in the cab, mate,' and I got back behind the wheel, and that's when the gent decided to hire me after all."

"Nice work. And where did you take him?"

"Larmont's Hotel, sir. You know it?"

"On Half Moon Street, isn't it?"

"That's one entrance. The other's right through in Clarges Street. It's a favourite place for slipping shadowers, so after I dropped him I drove round slow to the other door, and there he was, getting into another cab. I tailed it to that big

Green Star garage in Crayville Place. He paid it off and went in, and I hung around unobtrusive-like till he come out again, driving a Rover 2000, number TPN 2385."

Kendrick made a note of the number and said, "You're good at this."

"Well, that's about all there is to it, sir. I followed the Rover as far as Marble Arch, but then he went belting off down the Bayswater Road, and for all I knew it might be first stop Beaconsfield or somewhere, so I thought I'd better get back and make my report. I hope it's satisfactory, sir."

"Very," said Kendrick. He rewarded the man appropriately and, when he had gone, looked up the index mark TPN in his A.A. Handbook. It was an East Sussex registration, he found; and that area is not reached by going west on the Bayswater Road—unless, perhaps, you realize that you are being tailed.

It was now halfpast six, so he set out on foot to call for Lynn Everett. She was one of the more comfortable girls to call for, he reflected—no family to be uneasily polite to, not even a chattering room-mate to endure. Her parents lived in rustic retirement somewhere, and she led a bachelor existence in a two-room mews flat off Smith Street. He arrived there with time in hand.

Lynn, wrapper-clad, bade him give himself a drink while she finished dressing, and he sat down with the final edition of the *Evening Post,* which he had bought on his way. The "Man Dead on Line" story had moved out of Late News into the regular columns, and in doing so had expanded. A ticket found on the body had indicated which train it had probably fallen from, but the cause of death had not yet been established, and the man was still unidentified. Police had by no means ruled out the possibility of foul play . . . The item was not, Kendrick felt, the best of foundations for an evening of carefree fun.

Ten minutes later Lynn joined him, looking almost adult

and highly huggable, so he swept her up in his arms and kissed her soundly. When at length he set her down she said, "Whee! What do you do for an encore?"

"Forgotten so soon?" said Kendrick, and was about to show her when she dodged smartly behind a chair.

"The question was purely rhetorical," she said. "I think we'd better be leaving for somewhere less private."

"Any preferences?"

"Chinese for choice, but I don't really mind."

"The rice paddies it shall be," said Kendrick, "and in Soho if you've no objections, for I've a call to make around there later on."

"Suits me," said Lynn, checking off the contents of her handbag. "Money—hankie—key. Comb—lipstick—compact."

"Cleansing cream?" Kendrick suggested. "Toothbrush?"

Lynn smiled at him indulgently. "If there's one thing I love more than your incurable optimism, Don," she said, "it's that delicate, romantic build-up you give a girl. Come on—I'm hungry."

They went to the Sampan in Dean Street, and ate and drank very well, but they reached the coffee and Grand Marnier without Kendrick's having had a chance to do much probing about Colombia. He was pondering how best to start, when Lynn said, "All right, Transparent—let's have it."

"Let's have what?"

"You want some kind of information, don't you? But you can't think how to phrase your questions without letting me guess that that was your sole reason for taking me out."

"Not by a mile, it wasn't. My main reason was purely hedonistic—I wanted to have a really enjoyable evening on my first night back."

Lynn smiled, and said, "Thank you, Don. I know you're fibbing, but it still makes me feel good."

"That," said Kendrick, "is the story of my life. I have this indefinable quality that not only makes girls feel good but also makes them stay good. Yes, I admit I had a slight ulterior motive, but it was very secondary."

"Shoot, then, and—subject always to the Official Secrets Act —I'll sing for my supper if I can."

"I wondered," said the journalist, "whether the Foreign Office happened to have heard any informed gossip about current political trends in Colombia."

Lynn's green eyes narrowed, and she looked at him oddly. "You've just come back from there," she fenced. "Last Sunday's column was all about it. How the Andes are still infested by bandits, and Alexander von Humboldt called Bogotà the Athens of America, and—"

"Exactly," said Kendrick. "The kind of superficial stuff you pick up in the course of a four-day visit, or even get in a guidebook. I was hoping you might know whether there were any subterranean currents a fly-by-night columnist simply wouldn't get wind of—to mix a metaphor."

Lynn thought for a minute or so. "It's no official secret," she said at last, "that most Latin American countries have something bubbling up most of the time, and that Colombia's no exception. Nor is it a secret that tension out there has been building for months. I'll go even further, and say that the stopper might blow out any day, though it's less easy to forecast which particular pressure might blow it; the Army again, after all these years, or the Communists after all these bombs, or perhaps a revival of Urquiza-type separatism; or even those bandits you wrote about. But that, I'm afraid, is all I can tell you, and a pretty poor return it is for a delightful meal. Still, I'll throw in a piece of advice that's worth its weight in chicken chow mien—if you care to take it."

"Yes?"

"If you've found—or think you've found—an English tie-up with Colombian politics, drop it fast, and go in for something relatively safe, such as Russian roulette."

Kendrick paid the bill, and they left the Oriental calm of

the Sampan for the bustling sidewalks of polyglot Soho. "Where do you have to make your call, Don?" asked the girl.

"Round the corner, in Old Compton Street. We'll get a cab, and—"

"A cab!" said Lynn scornfully. She slipped an arm through his, and started to walk.

"I thought you might not like being left standing outside the place. I'll be as quick as I can, but—"

"I don't mind standing outside places. But I hate sitting outside them when there's a little meter going click-click every few seconds. Time enough for a cab when you come out. What kind of place is it anyway? A restaurant?"

"No, a club. The Philoptic. Something to do with astronomy, maybe. At all events, I understand they have facilities for observing the movements of heavenly bodies . . . Here we are."

Lynn's eyes widened when she saw the showcase photographs, with their generous display of bosoms and behinds. "A strip joint, for goodness sake!" she said. "If that's how your mind is working tonight, Don, you can forget about cabs. We're going home in a bus."

"Scaredy-kitten!" said Kendrick, who knew, having learned it the hard way, that his companion was a skilled exponent of judo. (She was also, unexpectedly, a more than fair rifle-shot, for she had been brought up in the mountainous oil-lands of Northern Iraq, where the Kurds have a proverb that may be roughly rendered as *A girl's best friend is her Mauser*.)

He rang the club bell and a doorman opened up, eyeing his large form with suspicion. "Member?" he growled.

Kendrick shook his head. "But not a plain-clothes cop either," he said, and gave the man one of his cards. "I'd like a word with Mr. Buchanan." He was grudgingly admitted.

The manager proved to be a hairy Scot who clearly knew the value of good press relations. He made only a token show of reluctance to divulge Alberdi's home address as recorded in the club books, but he did add a word of warning. "Some of the addresses applicants give us may be phoney, Mr. Kendrick," he said. "We've neither the time nor the organisation to check them. Of course, if some comedian writes 'The Vatican' or the like we crack down, but . . ."

Kendrick assured him that he would hold the club guiltless if Alberdi's address proved false. Then, as he was being escorted to the door, he remembered something else he had wanted to ask. "Tell me," he said, "what does 'philoptic' mean anyway?"

"It's an intriguing name, isn't it?" said Buchanan. "I got it from an Oxford professor who used to come to my last place, in the Strand. He told me it was classical Greek for an eyeful, but I'm afraid I don't speak Greek myself, classical or pop."

Kendrick came out to the cool night air and found Lynn looking at the window of a delicatessen. She greeted him with her sweetest smile and said, "Seen any good shows lately?"

"Sorry if it seemed a long time," said the journalist, "but I could be on the trail of something." A cab drew up in response to his signal, and as he followed the girl into it he read out the address Buchanan had given him. "Fieldfare Court, Church Road, S.W.3, please."

"What was that again?" asked the cabbie, and when Kendrick repeated it he said, "Sorry. No such place."

"No Fieldfare Court?"

"No Church Road, guv'nor. Not there."

"You're quite sure?"

"Course I'm sure. That's my job. There's over twenty Church Roads in Greater London, but none of 'em's in S.W.3. You're sure it's not Old Church Street? Or W.3 or S.W.13? They've both got Church Roads."

"I see. I guess I got it wrong," said Kendrick flatly, and gave the man Lynn's address instead.

He felt the girl's hand rest lightly on his own. "End of trail, Don?" she asked sympathetically.

"End of trail, baby."

"I'm sorry," said Lynn. "Although, if you're poking into what I think you are, I'm also glad; because I like you better without a knife in your back."

Kendrick dismissed the cab at Lynn's mews, saw her into her flat, and then set out briskly for his own. He had walked less than twenty yards, however, when a large car with a policeman at the wheel overtook him and stopped. As the journalist came abreast of it a young man in a lounge suit emerged from the back. "Mr. Kendrick?" he enquired politely.

"Yes," said Kendrick, hoping the sinking feeling did not show in his tone.

"I'm a police officer, Mr. Kendrick—Dane is my name—and I'd like to ask you a few questions. Shall we go round to your flat? Or would you rather come down to Scotland Yard?"

SEVEN

Sitting beside Dane on the rear seat as the car purred softly along King's Road, Kendrick said, "How did you know where I was? Have you been tailing me, for some reason?"

"No, we haven't been tailing you," said the detective. "I'd been trying to phone you at intervals since seven o'clock, and then by sheer chance one of my chaps noticed a man who answered your description coming out of the Sampan with Miss Everett; so I drove to her place and waited for you to arrive."

"I hadn't realized," said Kendrick carefully, "that Miss Everett was—what's the official phrase?—'known to the police'."

Dane laughed, and said, "She's not, in the official meaning of the phrase, but she's quite well known to the Special Branch. We work pretty closely with Foreign Office Security."

"The Special Branch?" said Kendrick in surprise. Then something clicked into place in his mind, and he said, "In that case you must be Detective Chief-Inspector Dane?"

"Guilty," said Dane. "But let's leave the questions till we reach Castlemaine Court, shall we?"

Kendrick fell silent, pondering. That the police had connected him with Maguire so quickly was surprising enough, but that it was the Special Branch who were interested rather than the C.I.D. was even more so.

Under the lights of the flat Dane did not appear quite so youthful, though his curly hair and unlined face belied his near-forty years. He had an air of guileless innocence that fitted neither his rank nor his record, and Kendrick recalled a crime-reporting colleague's opinion of him. *If Antony*

Dane died, Khrushchev would have the most deceptive appearance on earth. "Can I offer you a drink?" he asked.

"No, thanks," said Dane. "But I wouldn't say no to some coffee."

"I believe I could use a cup myself," said Kendrick, and went into the kitchen to make it. When he returned, the detective was examining the rows of paperbacks on his shelves.

"You seem to be a real thriller fan," he commented.

Kendrick nodded. "When you live the dull, routine life of Fleet Street," he said, "you find yourself seeking any old kind of escape."

"Well, you've had quite a change from Fleet Street recently," said Dane. "I'm enjoying your series very much, I may say. When will the Cuban article be appearing?"

Kendrick raised his eyebrows. "It won't," he said. "I didn't visit Cuba."

"Really?" The Chief-Inspector seemed genuinely surprised. "I thought that must be where you'd met Joe Clancy."

A little warning bell rang at the back of Kendrick's brain, and he contrived a convincing frown of concentration. "I don't think I ever have," he said. "I don't even know who he is."

"Was," Dane corrected. "He fell off a train early this morning and landed on his head. Finding nothing on his person to identify him, Lancashire sent his dabs to the Yard to see if they happened to be on record. They were."

"And why did you think I might know him?"

"Because," said the detective, "among other odds and ends in his pockets, there was a slip of paper with your name and address on it."

There was nothing faked about Kendrick's look of surprise. "Well, what do you know!" he exclaimed.

"As you don't appear in the telephone directory he couldn't have copied it from that. We thought you might have given it to him, especially as you were travelling on the same train."

"Well, I didn't."

"Any idea where he could have got it, then?"

"If we were travelling on the same train, yes, I have. There's a name-and-address tag on each of my suitcases, and after I'd stowed them in my sleeper I walked up and down the platform for a while. He could easily have slipped in and read the tags."

"H'm," said Dane doubtfully. "Rather risky with the car attendant there, and the chance that you might come back any moment. Have you given your address to anyone lately?"

Kendrick had a very clear memory of giving it to Manuela over the phone the previous evening; but, though he was still in at least two minds about that delightful rattlesnake, he felt a chivalrous inclination to keep her out of this if he could. "One or two South Americans, I guess," he said vaguely.

Dane dropped the subject and reached for his briefcase. "The only photograph we have of Clancy," he said, "was taken just before World War II, when he was in his early twenties. But one of our artists has done a sketch, based partly on it and partly on Lancashire's picture of the corpse. Does it suggest anyone to you?" He handed over a sheet of drawing-paper.

Kendrick caught his breath, and realized that there was no hope of bluffing. "Your art man's good," he said. "Put a dog-collar on this guy and he's Father Maguire. And you say he's dead? Well, well!"

"Father Maguire, eh? Come to think of it, Clancy studied for the priesthood at one time, but luckily he was found out and kicked out sharpish. Where did you meet him, Kendrick?"

"We were fellow-passengers on the *Duchess of Malfi* all week. As a matter of fact, I met him as seldom as possible. He never stopped talking."

"He's stopped now," said Dane gently, "so I think you'd better start."

"I beg your pardon?"

"Why did he have this address in his pocket? What was your connexion with him?"

"I didn't have any."

Dane gazed at him reproachfully. "I know I look a mug," he said, "but it still hurts to be taken for one."

Kendrick had been mentally marshalling his facts and running a blue pencil through those that seemed likely to give a lead to Manuela. Now he said, "Dane, could you bear to hear a story that's already made two people call me a liar?"

The Yard man's beam of pleasure seemed really genuine. "I'd love to," he said.

"On Tuesday night a private eye named Farrell went off the *Duchess of Malfi* into eternity. The Scottish police think he fell; the Captain thinks he was pushed. By me. But both the Captain and the police are agreed that, whatever may have happened, my version of it didn't."

"A promising start," said Dane approvingly. "I'm going to enjoy this."

Kendrick told the story just as he had told it to Captain Nicholson, but when he came to Farrell's mysterious companion he said, "All I could see of this other person was a flapping black skirt, so I took it to be a woman in evening dress, with her feet and ankles screened by Farrell's body. Later, when I learned from the police that not one woman passenger had worn evening dress that night, I wondered if it could possibly have been Father Maguire's soutane. Now I'm convinced it was."

"What convinced you?"

"You did, by telling me he not only wasn't a priest but also had a record at Scotland Yard. Now, if he and Farrell were engaged in some funny business—"

"Did you follow them up to the other deck?"

"No, I didn't, because at that moment . . . well, my original impression was that somebody coshed me, but the Captain and the Inspector poured such scorn on it that now I'm a little doubtful myself. Maybe their theory's right, and I was simply blown off my feet and hit my head on something. Either way, I woke up in hospital; and Farrell was never seen again."

"So?"

"So maybe that supplies a reason for Maguire's—sorry, Clancy's having my address in his pocket. If he and Farrell were partners in some deal he may have shared Farrell's interest in my private life. Alternatively, he may have shared the Captain's belief that I killed Farrell, and have been intending to call round here and avenge his buddy, when he'd have a great big city to melt away into instead of a comparatively small ship. Take your pick. But he had ample opportunity on board to get my address from the baggage-tags."

"You don't know why Farrell was interested in you?"

Kendrick hesitated, then said, "Directly, no. But I got it third-hand from the Captain that it was because I'd been in Colombia for a few days."

Dane nodded as if this made sense to him. "If you've recently been accused," he said thoughtfully, "of shoving a fellow-passenger off a ship, I suppose it would be rather unkind to ask if you threw another one out of a train; and fortunately I'm not investigating Clancy's death anyway. What interests me is his life, and what he would have done with it if it had gone on a little longer. You've told me how he came into this country, and I'm grateful, but I'd be even more grateful if you would tell me why."

The journalist shrugged. "I would if I knew," he said. "Dane, may I ask a question for a change?"

"Certainly."

"What was Clancy's line of business? Private eye, like Farrell?"

"Far from it. In his mis-spent youth he was a member of the self-styled Irish Republican Army, a group of terrorists who've caused a good deal of trouble in Britain and Ulster from time to time. Early in 1939 he was convicted of blowing up a bridge near London, and sentenced to ten years. That's when we got the photograph and dabs. After his release we lost trace of him for a while, but he showed up in various countries later on. The last fix we had on him was about a year ago. He was in Cuba, training saboteurs; a specially selected batch of them from Colombia . . . Well, Kendrick, if you're quite sure there's nothing more you can tell me about the chap . . ."

"Not a thing, I'm afraid," said the journalist, trying to hide his relief. Was it really over so easily?

"Then I may as well be getting along," said Dane, rising. Kendrick accompanied him to the outside door, where the Yard man halted abruptly. "Oh, by the way," he said, "have you got a gun licence?"

"Not I," said Kendrick. "But then I don't tote a gun."

"I see. So it was somebody else who was a trifle off target today?"

Kendrick's stomach went down like an express lift. "I—I don't get it," he said.

"Bullet in the window-frame," Dane explained, and the journalist realized that more than his books had been under inspection while he was making the coffee. "Absence of dust in the hole suggests that it hadn't been there very long. I'm afraid I made rather a mess digging it out." He produced a small nickel-jacketed object from his pocket and said, "Only seven millimetre, but even so, you're lucky it missed you . . . Kendrick, may I give you a word of advice?"

Kendrick, quite beyond speech, merely nodded.

"You're obviously a fellow who doesn't like reporting things to the police," said the detective, "so—put some putty in that hole and paint it over before the C.I.D. come round to talk about Clancy. These chaps have the nastiest, most suspicious minds in the business." He flashed Kendrick a friendly smile. *"Hasta luego,"* he said. "We'll be meeting again, I don't doubt."

For the third night in a row Kendrick slept little. This time his insomnia was the result—intended and achieved—of Antony Dane's carefully staged exit. "Leave 'em with something to worry about" seemed to be the detective's motto, and he had certainly done it with Kendrick.

The facetious advice about hiding the bullet-hole had conveyed its message with pellucid simplicity: a man who doesn't report being shot at won't trouble to report an embarrassing corpse—not if he can get rid of it instead. Kendrick cursed his failure to search the body first. If only he had found that tell-tale slip of paper—an *aide-memoire,* no doubt, in case the train attempt failed and another had to be made—the police might never have linked him with Clancy-Maguire at all.

Still, the damage was done, and for the moment there was nothing he could do but turn on his other side and try to sleep. Count sheep jumping over a gate. Count Farrells jumping over a taffrail. Count cops jumping over a columnist, but not quite making it. Count corpses jumping over train window-sills and landing on their heads. Count . . .

A sudden chill went through him. Just how certain was he that Clancy really had been a corpse when he went through that window?

Dane had spoken as if it was landing on his head that had killed him—and Dane had most probably known the result of the autopsy by that time. Suppose Clancy's collapse hadn't been a heart attack at all, but a fit! Not an epileptic one, that other kind—yes, cataleptic. Wasn't that the death-like one, the one where the body became cold and pale, with pulse and respiration virtually imperceptible? The one Poe used in *The Fall of the House of Usher?* If Clancy hadn't in fact died till he hit the tracks, then legally . . .

Kendrick ran a damp palm over his damp brow and tried to banish the memory of that quiet thud as the Irishman landed. He must get to sleep if he wasn't going to be a wreck by morning. Sleep. He remembered "Family Doctor" of the *Bulletin* a few months back, bringing his ripe Hippocratic wisdom to bear on the subject of insomnia.

First try to rid the mind of worry, the old fool had written, *for this is perhaps the greatest single obstacle to slumber.* Gee, thanks, Doc. Give a guy a cataleptic fit, drop him on the tracks on his head, feel the hot breath of Scotland Yard on your nape, and then rid the mind of worry. Damn you for an impractical theorist, Doc. And double-damn Antony Dane!

EIGHT

When the phone rang Kendrick blinked at the instrument for a few seconds, then lifted the receiver and muttered his name.

"This is Lynn," said the other end. "I hope I didn't wake you."

"As a matter of fact you did," said Kendrick, "in the nick of time. I don't seem to dream so good these nights. And what can I do for you this bright and beautiful morning? Or is it afternoon?"

"It's 9.30 a.m., it's Sunday, and I wanted to catch you before you went out. Don, is there any chance of my seeing you, even for half an hour or so? Somewhere quiet, where we can talk?"

Shortly before falling asleep at daybreak, Kendrick had resolved not to stay at home and wait for the C.I.D. If they wanted him they would find him quickly enough, and in the meantime there were better things to do with a holiday than pace the floor of a small flat, gnawing your nails. "Sure is," he said. "Let's have a day up the river or someplace; starting soonest, as they say in telegrams."

"That," said Lynn, "will be very nice indeed. Leave your door unlatched and I'll come round and make your breakfast while you're dressing. It'll save time."

Kendrick thanked her, and did as he was bidden. By the time he had tubbed and shaved there were promising noises in the kitchen, and when he finally emerged from his bedroom the air was rich with the scent of coffee and kippers. He joined Lynn, patted her shapely stern as she stooped to look under the grill, and said, "How did a nice girl like you ever come to take up judo?"

Lynn grinned and said, "You're your own best answer. Go away and sit down, Don. I'm about to serve."

Later, when he had largely assuaged his appetite, he said, "Well, what did you want to see me about?"

A shadow crossed the piquant little face. "Don't rush me, Don," said the girl. "We've got hours ahead of us. Let's enjoy some of them before we get serious."

"Okay, if you prefer it. Do you happen to have seen a paper this morning? Not having been at the office last night, I don't have one."

"Yes, I've seen the *Bulletin*. They ran your Paraguayan piece."

"Is there anything new on that chap who was found dead on the railroad in . . . was it Lancashire?"

"It was Lancashire," said Lynn, giving him an inscrutable look. "He has now been identified as Joseph Eamon Clancy, believed to be a native of Eire. An inquest will be held on Monday, but pending the coroner's verdict the police are treating the investigation as a murder one."

"The heck they are," said Kendrick in dismay.

"That's what it said. They've issued a description of the dead man, and asked anyone who saw him on the train to come forward. More coffee?"

"I don't think so, thanks. Let's not waste the sunshine. Let's dump the dishes in the sink and take off."

They rode the lift down to the basement garage, climbed into Kendrick's Humber Super Snipe, and drove up the ramp and round the corner into King's Road. There certainly wasn't a cordon round the building, nor even a parked patrol car with its hawk-eyed crew on watch; and he saw nothing among the many vehicles in his rear-view mirror that looked particularly like a tail. For the prime suspect in a murder investigation, he thought, he was being surprisingly neglected. Long might it continue.

He took a zigzag course through Chelsea and Kensington to Notting Hill, then headed west on the Uxbridge Road. Acton fell behind, and Ealing and Southall, and by that time he was pretty certain that he was not being followed. Some of his gloom fell from him, and he started to count his blessings: a sunny day, a growing thirst, a smooth-running car, and a passenger he was really fond of. He found himself humming the tune his car radio was playing. "Happy?" his passenger enquired.

"Mphm. But I'd be happier still if you'd burst your little bombshell and clear the air."

"Not while you're driving," said the girl. "I want you to be looking me in the face when we talk."

"From as close a range as you like," said Kendrick cheerfully, "such as point blank. I'm not scared."

From Uxbridge he took the Windsor road through Iver Heath, admiring the autumn shades of the trees and wondering what masterpieces of screen art might be a-making at the near-by Pinewood Studios. They were in Buckinghamshire now, but only briefly, for at Slough he turned west again into Berkshire. As they drove through Maidenhead without stopping, Lynn said, "Wargrave, by any chance?"

"Unless you'd prefer Skindles?"

"No, thanks. It'll probably be packed on a day like this, and anyway I like Wargrave. Remember the last time you took me there?" Her eyes were laughing.

"No," said Kendrick firmly, "I do not. And I don't want to be reminded of it, either. The secret of success is to forget one's defeats."

"Then why are we re-visiting the battlefield?"

"Because the beer's good," said Kendrick truthfully.

They drank it on the riverside lawn of the St. George & Dragon, then went within for lunch. After it, Kendrick hired a punt and, with Lynn reclining comfortably on cushions, poled it ahead with long, easy strokes. Soon he turned the square bows out of the current, and Lynn raised her eyebrows and said, "Isn't this the same backwater that—"

"The backwater is the same," said Kendrick, giving a final thrust with the pole and then shipping it, "but the mood and the motive are not. We are now, Miss Everett, in about as quiet a spot as we're likely to find. So out with the bad news." He ducked to dodge an overhanging branch, and sat down.

Lynn thought for a moment and then said, "I had a visitor this morning; Tony Dane of the Special Branch. He said he had been talking to you last night. He's worried, Don."

"*He's* worried? What does he think *I* am?"

"He thinks you're holding out on him. He thinks you know far more about Joseph Eamon Clancy than you admit."

"Does he also think I killed the guy, or didn't he mention that?"

Lynn's eyes widened. "Did you kill him?" she asked.

"I'm waiting for the coroner to tell me. I like to think I didn't."

"For God's sake, Don! What on earth have you been up to?"

"It's a long story, babe. What else does Dane think?"

"That Clancy was probably working for the Colombian communists, that you know what he was doing in England, and that you're pigheadedly risking an international incident such as the Colombian Embassy being blown up by one of his colleagues, simply because you hope to beat Scotland Yard to it, handle the thing yourself, and get a scoop for your paper."

"Dane really believes that?"

"As far as I know. And he's not happy about it."

"I'll bet he's not. But why should he pick on you to share his troubles?"

Lynn's lips curled in her familiar, self-deriding grin. "He saw you embracing me ardently at the door last night," she said, "after you brought me home from the Sampan. And, as

he's apparently unaware that you're Canada's answer to Casa-
nova, he attached undue significance to the incident. Where-
fore he hoped I could induce you to come clean, and let the
professionals take charge before you'd mucked up the whole
operation. I assured him that I had no influence over you at all,
but I promised I'd at least try." She looked at him pleadingly.
"You do know more than you told him, don't you? About
Clancy, I mean."

"It's really only guesswork."

"Well, please tell him whatever it is, and don't try to go it
alone. *Please!*"

"Why don't you tell him yourself?"

The girl looked bewildered. "Tell him what?" she asked
blankly.

"Last night, Lynn, you advised me to run for cover if I
found an English tie-up with Colombian politics. Were you
simply making conversation, or did you perhaps have some
slight inkling of why Clancy was in this country?"

Lynn shook her head vigorously. "On my word of honour,
Don," she said, "I never heard of Clancy till this morning, and
I haven't the slightest idea what he was doing here. The tie-up
I had in mind . . . well, I can't talk about it, and it may not
even exist, but . . . anyway, it couldn't have anything to do
with communists. Darling, please tell Dane whatever it is that
you know. Or guess."

Kendrick was silent for a time, weighing things. At last he
said, "Right now, honey, I'm not very fond of the police—particularly Dane, who kept me awake all night. Furthermore, I'm
too darn worried about how that inquest goes tomorrow to
have much time for other people's problems. However, you've
kept your word and made your pitch and I'll think it over; but
not until the sword of Damocles has either fallen or been
sheathed. And now I'd like to forget the whole business for as
long as events will allow. Care to help me?"

The afternoon passed pleasantly, but by five o'clock fog

patches were beginning to form, and Kendrick decided to get on the road before it became any more dense. From Wargrave he drove north through Marlow, where the fog was considerably thicker; but it thinned again as they left the immediate vicinity of the Thames, and by the time they reached High Wycombe there was none. At the Bull's Head in Aylesbury they dined well on one of the famous local ducks, then set off on the last leg to London. Twenty miles out they ran into fog again, as yet more of a threat than a blanket, but thick enough to make driving slow and irksome. And at length, after a wholly uneventful trip, the Humber pulled up outside Lynn's flat.

Kendrick looked at his watch and said, "I suppose it's too late for you to offer me some hot milk, or show me your etchings, or whatever?" He had realized that he did not want to be alone with his thoughts any sooner than he had to.

Possibly Lynn sensed his mood, for she said, "We-ell . . . All right, for a little while. Just this once."

They went into her flat and she made Bovril, and they drank it, and talked of everything under the sun except Clancy and Dane and the morrow. But at eleven o'clock Lynn said firmly, "Time up, Don. We've already given that old witch across the way enough material for a week's whispering."

"She's not home," said the journalist, "or else she's gone to bed. I particularly noticed that her apartment was dark."

"That means she's there," said Lynn confidently. "When she goes out in the evening she leaves the lights on to fool burglars. Dark windows mean she's peeping round a curtain at the wickedness of the world. She never goes to bed. So scram."

As Kendrick stepped out into the mews he looked searchingly in both directions, but saw no sign of lurking cops or even of parked cars other than his own. It was odd, he felt, that Scotland Yard had apparently lost interest in him so suddenly. Maybe, of course, it hadn't. Maybe he just wasn't as good at spotting shadowers as he thought he was.

He slid in behind the wheel of the Humber and switched on the ignition. As he did so he sensed rather than heard a movement behind him, but before he could turn, something pricked the back of his neck and a voice murmured, "Sit still, Kendrick, or I'll skewer you. It's a fifteen centimetre blade." In the rearview mirror he saw a dark shape rise from the floor and settle on the back seat, all without taking the knife from his neck. The man's features were indistinguishable, but the voice was the voice of Alberdi.

"And now we'll go for a little drive together," said the Latin, "but before we start I'd better warn you not to try to attract police attention by speeding or crashing red lights or anything. You'll die rather painfully if you do."

"And you'll walk away from the wreckage unscathed and unpursued?"

"Probably not, but . . . Kendrick, I think it would help if you understood my position. The people I work for don't tolerate failure, and agents who fall down on the job are dealt with very promptly. If you hadn't killed Clancy, someone else would have done it; and I too failed yesterday morning, as you know, so I'm living on borrowed time. I am therefore perhaps readier to risk my life than you are to risk yours, for mine is already forfeit if I don't redeem myself pretty quickly."

There was something in his voice that carried conviction, and the point of the knife was very sharp. "Where do I drive to?" asked Kendrick.

"Straight through the mews, and turn left. Then I'll direct you."

Without answering, Kendrick started the car and drove off slowly into the fog.

NINE

Lynn Everett slid yawning into bed, snuggled under the sheets, and reached out to switch off the light; but the phone rang, so she lifted the receiver instead.

"Miss Everett?" queried a high-pitched female voice that she could not place.

"Speaking."

"I do apologize for phoning at this hour, Miss Everett, and probably it's none of my business, but I saw that your light was still on, and—"

"Who's speaking, please?"

"Oh! Oh yes, of course. This is Emma Sankey, Miss Everett. You know—in number eight, across the mews."

"Yes, Miss Sankey?" Lynn tried not to sound too icy.

"As I say, it's really none of my business, I suppose, but— that young man who brought you home tonight—Mr. Kendrick, isn't it?—had he arranged to meet somebody in the mews when he left, do you know?"

An unpleasant feeling assailed the pit of Lynn's stomach. She remembered how loth Don had been to leave, and said, "No, I'm quite sure he hadn't. What happened?"

"Well, I just chanced to see you arriving home, and as soon as you and Mr. Kendrick had gone indoors another man came along and got into the back of Mr. Kendrick's car."

"And—and then?"

"Well, nothing. I supposed it was someone he had offered a lift to, or—"

"It wasn't. What happened when he went out?"

"He got into the driving-seat, and then nothing happened at all for a long time. I mean, he didn't even switch on the inside light, which is what made me think it all rather unusual. And then he just drove away, with the other man still in the back seat. I couldn't make up my mind whether to phone you or—"

"I'm very glad you did, Miss Sankey. Thank you. And—I shouldn't go to bed right away, if I were you. I think we may have the police round shortly."

She broke the connexion, then dialled Scotland Yard and asked for the Special Branch duty officer. "Lynn Everett of F.O. Security here," she said crisply when a Sergeant Wood came on the line. "Unless the police have made a rather unusual type of arrest, I think Don Kendrick of the *Sunday Bulletin* has been abducted from outside my flat." She gave chapter and verse, including the number of the Super Snipe, and ended, "Chief-Inspector Dane is interested in Mr. Kendrick at present, so—"

"I'll get word to him right away, Miss Everett. That was no arrest. Where can I ring you back?"

Lynn told him her phone number, hung up and started to dress. She had just finished when Wood rang. "Is Mr. Dane there yet?" he asked.

"No. Is he coming himself?"

"Yes. Perhaps you'd be good enough to tell him that I've checked with Castlemaine Court, and Mr. Kendrick has not returned there, so I've put out a general call for his car."

Lynn said she would, and five minutes later she did. Dane said, "Thanks. Who and where is this eye-witness, Lynn?" She told him, and he said, "I'll be back when I've talked to her. Please don't go to bed."

Go to bed, for Heaven's sake! With Don missing and possibly murdered by this time! What did Dane think she was? She walked around restlessly, lifting things and laying them down again, biting her lip, and generally showing such signs of agitation that Kendrick, could he have seen her, would have been amazed. For Kendrick's first acquaintance with Lynn had been made in a context of violence. He had seen her unperturbed under gunfire, quietly resigned to the prospect of imminent death, and he would have found this fluttering creature difficult to credit.

Perhaps the explanation was that she found danger easier to take than inactivity. Perhaps, again, it was something else altogether. Who can tell what motivates a redhead? Frequently, not even the redhead herself.

By the time Dane returned she was calmer, and had even brewed some tea. He gratefully accepted a cup and said, "Nothing very much from Miss Sankey—simply a description that would fit half the men in London. But we can't really blame her, I suppose, with such poor visibility. We ought to be grateful that she was watching at all, and had sufficient curiosity to phone you about it."

"Curiosity?"

"Yes. She's dying to know what it's all about. I think she rather hoped that Mr. X was a rival for your affections, and that he and Kendrick had gone off to slug it out somewhere. Tell me, to change the subject, did you have any luck with Kendrick today?"

The girl shook her head. "None," she admitted. "He promised he would think it over, but not till he knew for sure whether he'd . . . well, he was waiting for the result of an— an enquiry."

Dane looked at her in surprise. "Not the Clancy inquest?" he asked.

"Well . . . yes. When he heard that the police were treating it as murder, he . . ."

"Naturally thought he'd be charged with it," said Dane. "Blast! The C.I.D. put that out to give the case a sense of urgency and encourage any potential witnesses to come forward, but they knew quite well it wasn't. Clancy died of a heart attack; but he almost certainly did it in the course of a fight with Kendrick, who then lugged the body down the corridor—shamming drunk for the benefit of a lady who happened to see him—and pitched it out onto the line."

Lynn was staring at him wide-eyed. "But why?" she demanded.

"Because he's either involved in something crooked or trying to get involved in it, and doesn't want the police buzzing round. Did he tell you that someone tried to shoot him in his flat on Saturday?"

"He did not," said Lynn. "Is it true?"

"Well, I suppose it was Kendrick they were trying to shoot. I happened to find the bullet. Yes, I'm afraid your young man is mixing with some rather violent types these days." Dane glanced at his watch, said, "Lynn, I . . ." He cleared his throat, avoided her eye, and said, "Please don't misunderstand me, but—I imagine you're fairly well known to the staff at Castlemaine Court?"

The girl smiled and said, "Oh, yes. I go in and out quite brazenly, believe it or not. Never tiptoe down the fire-escape at all."

Dane reddened. "I meant that they know you as an old friend of Kendrick's," he said, "so they might . . . What I want to do is get into his flat, but I don't want to make a production of it by using a search-warrant—not till I have some idea of what's happened to him."

"I could probably persuade the night porter to let me in—tell him I think I left my office keys there this morning and I need them for tomorrow. I'm game to try, anyway, if you think it may help us to find Don."

"I don't know whether it will or not," said the detective honestly, "but it can't hinder, and it may do some good."

Dane was driving his own Hillman, and they made good time through the fog-muffled streets to the apartment block. The porter in charge was Howard, a fortunate chance, for he had long approved of Lynn. He accepted the yarn she had concocted, and the three of them went up together in the lift. Howard unlocked the door of 607 with his pass-key, stepped inside to switch on the lights, and said, "Mother of God!"

The hall was a mess, and the lounge looked like a "tail-end-of-hurricane" photo from Florida. Everything that could be moved had been moved. Books lay everywhere, furniture had been ripped, pictures were on the floor with their backs off, the desk drawers lay around empty amid a scatter of their former contents, cushions had been opened and their stuffing poured out. . . . It was sheer devastation.

The bedroom was as bad, and in the kitchen not only had everything been taken off the shelves, but every container had been emptied onto the floor, leaving it carpeted with tea, coffee, sugar, cereals, detergent and Heaven knew what else. The only things that seemed to have been untouched, Lynn noticed with a lump in her throat, were the breakfast dishes, still standing forlornly in the sink where she had stacked them.

"Lunatic vandalism!" said Howard. It was about the fourth time he had said it, but this time Dane replied.

"I don't think so, no," he said. "Howard, I hadn't meant to mention this, but I'm a detective, looking into the possible disappearance of Mr. Kendrick." He held out his warrant-card for inspection. "Will you please go down to the main doors and stand by to admit the local police when they arrive? I'm going to phone them now."

He returned to the bedroom, wrapped his handkerchief round the receiver and dialled, saying, "Don't touch anything, Lynn. I'm going to have the place gone over for finger-prints."

"You'll find plenty of mine in the kitchen," said Lynn dully. "I made Don's breakfast this morning. Yesterday morning, to be strictly accurate. Sunday."

"And then you went out together for the day?"

"Yes."

"What time did . . . ah! This is Chief-Inspector Dane of the Special Branch, speaking from Flat 607, Castlemaine

Court, King's Road." He went on quickly and concisely, listened for a few moments, said, "Good," and hung up.

"We left here about halfpast ten, or a little after," said the girl.

"Did you come back at all?"

She shook her head, and Dane nodded. "So they could have done this at any time during the day. Wonder what they were looking for. A letter or a photograph or some other flat thing, presumably—otherwise why take the backs off picture-frames?" He browsed around, while Lynn sat on the ruins of the bed and gazed about her miserably.

"This suggest anything to you?" said Dane, holding up the journalist's dinner-jacket.

"They thought something might be hidden in the lining."

"Think so? Look again."

She did, and sat up. "Something had been; but Don had taken it out again. The people who wrecked this place wouldn't have wasted time unpicking stitches, they'd have slashed it."

"Good girl. And once he'd removed it, where do you suppose he would hide it for greater safety?"

"I've no idea, but if it was anywhere in the flat they must have found it."

"Agreed, practically. So, to jump to a conclusion, they didn't find it, and that's why they snatched him—to see if he was carrying it about with him."

The door-bell rang, and Dane admitted three men with a flash-camera and other equipment. Dane and Lynn gave their finger-prints for elimination purposes, and then the men went to work on the flat. Dane left them to it, and he and Lynn went down to rejoin Howard the porter.

Here the detective struck lucky, for Howard explained that this was only the start of his night-duty month and that he had been on the day shift on Saturday. Yes, Mr. Kendrick had had a visitor—within minutes of his return from foreign parts. The porter described "Gomez" and, under questioning, recalled the journalist's initial unwillingness to talk to him; the Latin's claim to have urgent business connected with Kendrick's transatlantic crossing; and the incident of the crash that had alarmed the lady in the flat below. Mr. Gomez, he added, had left soon after this incident, apparently in a hurry.

Other visitors? Well, he wasn't sure whether the second man had been visiting Mr. Kendrick or somebody else in the block, for he hadn't seen him till he was leaving, but Mr. Kendrick had certainly been very interested in him. Howard described John Doe in detail, and told of the steps the journalist had taken to have him shadowed. No, he was sorry, he did not know what report the cab-driver had made to Kendrick, but the man's name was Alf Groves and he would no doubt be on the rank again in the morning.

Dane pocketed his Parker, snapped the elastic on his notebook, and said, "Thanks. Now, Lynn, shall I drive you home, or would you like to come down to the Yard with me and see what's happening?"

"I think," said Lynn uncertainly, "I think I'd like to go to the Yard with you. Yes, please, the Yard." She stepped out quickly into the fog, hoping that Dane had not noticed the worry she knew her face must be revealing.

At the Yard Sergeant Wood handed his chief a slip of paper and said, "Came in ten minutes ago, sir." Dane read it, turned to the girl and looked at her gravely.

"Kendrick's car's been found in Fulham," he said, "so it hadn't gone very far." He saw the unspoken question in her eyes and shook his head. "No sign of a struggle—no blood or anything—but no sign of Kendrick either. Do you want to hang around here on the off-chance that something more may come in, or would you rather go home?"

"Which are you doing?"

"Going home, but if you want to wait I'll arrange for a car to—"

"No, thanks, I'd rather go with you, if you don't mind."

"Good," said Dane, and turned to the Sergeant. "Woody, get onto Traffic, will you, and get the address of a cab-driver called Alf Groves, number unfortunately unknown, but he works off that rank beside Castlemaine Court. He did a tailing job for Kendrick on Saturday afternoon. I want someone on his doorstep at dawn to get full details of it."

"Right, sir," said Wood, making a note.

"I also want someone at the Webster Line office at opening time to check the passenger list for the *Duchess of Malfi*'s latest west-east crossing, with particular reference to a passenger named Gomez, if any; especially interesting would be an address in this country, if they have one." He gave a few further instructions, then opened the door and held it ajar. "Let's go, Lynn," he said. "And cheer up. Things may not be as black as you think." She sensed pity in his voice, and was annoyed. Tony Dane was too observant by half.

Back once more in her own flat, she flopped into a chair and reviewed the night's happenings. She was angry with herself for having let slip Don's fears about the inquest, even more angry with Don for his duplicity at the Sampan. Why hadn't he told her right out that he was already up to his long ears in Colombian political intrigue, throwing red saboteurs off trains, hiding mysterious objects in his dinner jacket, and being shot at in his own flat? And that moreover he had every intention of getting in even deeper if he could? Who did the big oaf think he was? Superman?

Something would have to be done about Don, she decided, but at the moment she was too bushed to think just what, or how. Wearily she took off her clothes and went back to bed.

TEN

The story of Kendrick's experiences that night, as he later told it himself, bore so little relation to the truth that it might be well to go back some hours and find out what really did happen.

He drove the Humber, as directed, to a quiet cul-de-sac in Fulham, and was there transferred at knife-point to an Austin saloon. Alberdi again took the rear seat, while his prisoner sat in front with the driver—a silent, fur-coated figure who smelled attractively of Chanel 5. The Austin moved off.

Kendrick peered out into the murk in hopes of memorizing their route, but the driver seemed to know her London well enough to avoid the major landmarks, and they zigzagged through a maze of foggy back streets that defied recognition. He considered for a time the chances of whipping open the door and jumping out, but a tentative grope to locate the handle brought instant warning in the shape of a jab in the neck and a muttered, "Don't try it!" from the back seat. He gave up the idea.

After an age he glimpsed through the gloom a gracefully curving rail, and knew that they were crossing Hammersmith Bridge. Then there was an absence of lights that suggested Barnes Common, then more quiet streets that led to a second glimpse of the curving rail. They were again crossing Hammersmith Bridge. Kendrick abandoned hope of learning the route and stopped straining his eyes.

It was well into the small hours when the tyres crunched on gravel and the headlamps lit up an empty garage. The car rolled to rest inside, and the driver, switching off the engine, slipped from her seat. Kendrick heard the garage door clang shut, and then a light came on. "Get out," said Alberdi, "and do it slowly, with your hands in full sight. My colleague has you covered, and there's nobody near enough to hear a shot." Kendrick obeyed orders.

The driver, seen in the unshaded light of the garage, proved to be thirtyish and extremely pretty in a dimpled way, though the little gun in her hand detracted somewhat from her charm. Kendrick wondered if it was a twin of the *Cabrito* he had captured, or if Alberdi had somehow recovered his property. He did not bother to ask.

The two marched him through an inside door into an uncarpeted stone passage, then down six steps to a large, badly lit semi-basement that seemed to serve several purposes, for it contained a furnace, a washing-machine, garden tools, and a carpenter's work-bench. Alberdi, who had taken over the gun, motioned Kendrick to the middle of the room and, standing well clear of him, said, "Strip!"

"I beg your pardon?"

"I satisfied myself today, Kendrick, that the papers are not in your apartment. I'm now going to find out if they're on your person."

"They're not."

"I'll check for myself. As you take off each garment, toss it over there on the floor. Any tricks, and I'll search your corpse instead. So strip."

Kendrick shrugged and started to undress. "How Philoptical can you get?" he murmured. "I trust you're a married woman, ma'am."

For the first time the driver spoke. "Twice over," she said tersely. She sounded English.

When Kendrick had nothing on but his wrist-watch Alberdi said, "Right. Now lie face downwards on the floor."

"For Pete's sake!"

"No, for your own." The trigger-finger tightened, and the journalist lay down. Both Alberdi and his partner, he felt, were barely suppressing incipient jitters, and he did not wish to risk an eruption of nerves.

"Shall I hold the gun while you tie him, Primo?" asked the woman.

Primo hesitated for a moment, then said, "No. If there's going to be any shooting it had better be accurate. I'll hold it while you tie him. And if he tries to use you as a shield, God help him." He moved a couple of paces nearer his target and said, "Carry on, Kitty."

Five minutes later Kendrick's wrists were bound behind his back with window-cord, his ankles were tied together with another length of it, and a balled-up handkerchief was quite effectively gagging him. Throw in the cold concrete floor for good measure, and he had seldom felt less comfortable in his life.

Alberdi gathered up the discarded garments and said, "If we find the papers you have nothing to worry about. If we do not . . . well, I'm sure we can persuade you to tell us where they are." The pair disappeared from the prisoner's range of vision and he heard the door close and a key turn.

Not without difficulty he contrived to sit up, half expecting to find his captors watching him derisively; but no, they really had gone out of the room. How long it would take them to search his clothes and then come back for the torture session he could not guess. Not very long, probably. He would have to work fast.

"You may have been a bride twice over, Kitty, but you weren't a Girl Guide even once," he muttered to the gag with some satisfaction. "I'll bet you can't even tie parcels properly." While the woman was binding him he had, of course, strained hard against the cord, so that now his bonds were relatively slack. He worked the wrist ones off first, untied and spat out his gag, and then released his ankles. The entire process had taken little longer than the tying-up.

Guaranteed half an hour or so to work in, he thought, he could take one of the ventilators out of the wall and crawl through into the garden or whatever lay outside. But it seemed improbable that he would be left alone so long, and he could not afford to be caught off guard. It would be safer to await their return before trying to escape. He examined the tool-rack above the work-bench, selected a well balanced claw-hammer, and took up his position behind the door.

Cramp in the soles of both feet proved the worst feature of his unexpectedly long wait, but it had eased off by the time he again heard the key turn in the lock. He tensed himself, praying that Alberdi would be the first to enter, and raised the hammer. When the door began to open he jerked it with his left hand, stepped round the edge, saw the Latin gaping at him for a wide-eyed second; then struck.

As Alberdi slumped to the floor Kendrick ran up to the passage and looked both ways along it. There was no sign of Kitty, so he returned to the furnace-room and locked himself in with his unconscious victim. On the floor beside the man, dropped as he fell, lay a riding whip, a candle, tweezers, a bread-saw and a mousetrap. Improvising with the simple household goods to hand, Alberdi could have been very persuasive indeed.

Quickly Kendrick went through his pockets, finding the gun and then the wallet with the driving-licence and the girlie postcards. So Alberdi had recovered his property all right, no doubt in the course of satisfying himself that Manuela's papers were not in the apartment. Kendrick pictured the wreckage that he guessed would be waiting to welcome him home, and felt less regret than ever at having slugged the Latin with that hammer.

The fellow was breathing shallowly, and when Kendrick felt his wrist he found the skin cold and the pulse rapid. There was no knowing how soon the stupor might wear off, though, so to be on the safe side Kendrick tied him up with the window-cord he had recently worn himself. As he was completing the job someone tried the door-handle and then called, "Primo! Let me in!" It sounded like Kitty.

Gun in hand, the journalist unlocked the door, opened it and said, "Hi, Toots!" The woman stared at him unbelievingly; then, as she saw the bound figure on the floor, choked. "I was just going to start on him with the whip," said Kendrick pleasantly, "but since you're here I'll put on my clothes first. Lead me to them, please."

He wiggled the *Cabrito,* and without a word Kitty turned and walked up the stone stair. She had removed her fur coat, and her short pleated skirt swayed temptingly, but Kendrick reminded himself that there was a time and a place for everything. "You're Mrs. Alberdi, I take it?" he asked.

"No," said his captive, "I'm not." She was leading him through a well equipped kitchen now.

"Mrs. Who, then?"

"Does it matter?" They went down a thickly carpeted hall and into a biggish lounge.

"I always like to mention people's names in my stories," said Kendrick. "It gives them authenticity." He saw his clothes piled on a settee, and said, "Clasp your hands on the back of your neck and stand facing that wall till I get my things on."

"Aren't you modest!" said Kitty contemptuously, doing as instructed.

"Cautious is a better word," said Kendrick. "I can't dress with a gun in my hand, and I'd hate to be literally caught with my pants down."

"You mean you're afraid to tackle a woman unless you have a gun in your hand?" The scorn was even more obvious, and he guessed that she was trying to needle him.

"I mean that I may not be the only person with a gun. I haven't searched you, remember." He paused for effect, then added, "Yet." There was silence for the rest of the time it took him to dress.

"All right," he said at last, "you can turn round now. And have a seat, if you like."

Kitty turned, stumbled to a chair, and sat down as if her legs had given way. For all the scornful assurance with which she had spoken earlier, the look in her eyes was that of a terrified child. "What—what are you going to do?" she asked apprehensively.

Kendrick raised his eyebrows. "You can't guess?" he said. "I'm kidnapped, carried off to the Lord knows where, stripped, tied up, threatened with torture . . . What do you suppose I'm going to do? Invite you and Primo out for a night on the town?"

"You're . . . going to call the police? You wouldn't—wouldn't be willing just to forgive and forget?" Her attempt at a smile was not very successful.

"Why the heck should I?"

Her eyes fell, and she mumbled, "I thought perhaps I could . . . make a deal with you . . . I don't mean money." The faltering words trailed away, and her face went scarlet.

Kendrick looked at her almost gently. "Sorry, doll," he said, "but I've never yet blackmailed my way into a bed. Any other suggestions?"

The colour drained from her face, leaving it white. "None," she said hopelessly. "There's a phone in the study—across the hall."

"Suppose we talk a little before I use it. Is this your house, Primo's, or neither?"

"Mine."

"Where is it?"

"Datchet."

Kendrick grinned and said, "Twenty miles from Town! You sure took the long way home . . . Who are you?"

"Kitty Olsen. You possibly know my husband, Dick. He's a journalist too."

"I know him by repute," said Kendrick. This was making sense. Alberdi had indicated that he was working for the same people Clancy had served, which almost certainly meant some communist group; and Richard Olsen, editor of a left-wing review, was believed to be actively even farther left than his writings. "Where is he at the moment?"

"In Prague, covering the conference. He flew there on Friday. Otherwise he'd have helped Primo and I'd probably never have known anything about it. God, why did Dick have to go away and leave me to . . . to . . ."

Bit by bit, with a little prompting, the facts came out. Alberdi, who was a Cuban, had saved Olsen's life during a climbing expedition there, and Olsen had of course jumped at the chance of repaying the debt when Primo came to England on an assignment. He had not only made the man his house-guest for the duration of his stay, but had pledged full support from Kitty and himself in carrying out the mission.

And what exactly was the mission?

"I'm not quite sure of the details," said Kitty, "but some girl was coming to England with the plans for a revolt in Colombia, and the communists wanted to get hold of them so that they could make sure it wouldn't interfere with whatever it is that they're cooking up themselves. That may not be quite accurate, but I think it's fairly near. Anyway, they sent Primo to get the plans for them."

"How long has he been here?"

"Three weeks. Then on Friday night some colleague phoned him from Scotland to say that he was pretty sure it was now you who had them, and he'd try to get hold of them on the overnight train, but if he couldn't manage it he'd see Primo at Euston Station on Saturday morning and they'd arrange something else. So I drove Primo to Euston, but his colleague wasn't on the train after all. Primo recognized you from your description, though, and we followed you to Castlemaine Court. You know the rest."

Kendrick looked at her thoughtfully. "What I don't know," he said, "is where and to whom in England the Colombian girl was taking those papers. And why. Any idea?"

Kitty Olsen shook her head and said, "Not the slightest. I've told you absolutely everything I know. Mr. Kendrick, what's the penalty for kidnapping? Life?" Once again he was reminded of a terrified child.

"Haven't a clue," he said cheerfully. "But don't worry about it too much. I can't promise immunity for the Cuban heel, but maybe I'll be able to fix you up with an alibi or something. I've always been a sucker for dimples." He saw the light of hope return to her eyes, and said, "Now let's go see if Primo's recovered enough to stand a little quiet questioning, with or without the mousetrap and the tweezers. Ugh!"

Primo, however, had not recovered enough. He looked, indeed, rather worse. His face, previously pale, was now flushed, his pulse slow, his breathing stertorous; and no amount of shaking or slapping brought any sign of consciousness. If Kendrick had ever had any intention of calling in the police, the sight of Alberdi would have stopped him. The Clancy inquest was quite enough to have on one's plate at one time.

He looked gravely at Kitty. "This guy," he said, "needs medical attention, and pretty darn quick at that; which forces my hand, I'm afraid. I can't blow the whistle on him without giving you away too, so I'll simply have to let him go free. There never was a kidnapping, and I've never been in your house in my life."

She blinked moist eyes and said, "Mr. Kendrick, that's the most generous gesture—"

"Forget it," said Kendrick, feeling ashamed of his hypocrisy. "Now, you're the one who'll have to phone for a doctor, so listen and I'll give you the story you're going to tell."

"Half a sec. What happens if Primo tells a different one when he comes to?"

"Don't worry, he won't. Primo's no amateur. When he wakes up and finds he's not in jail he'll pretend he's lost his memory, and from then on he'll play it by ear. Okay. Now for your little piece." He started to untie Alberdi's bonds, talking as he did so.

He went on talking as he wiped his fingerprints off the claw-hammer and replaced it in the tool-rack; threw the window-cord onto the work-bench whence it had come; and gathered up the implements of torture. "These had better go back in their proper places before the doctor comes," he said, handing them to her. "Oh, did Primo have a drink recently, by any chance? I seemed to smell it."

"He had three stiff brandies before he went back to—to question you."

"Good. Work them into the story." Kendrick looked at his watch. "It's seven-fifteen," he said. "Let's allow half an hour for me to get well away from here and for you to put on your nightie and a robe before you discover the accident. I'm going to shift Alberdi into a better position. Run through your spiel while I'm arranging him, and try to make it sound convincing."

"Mr. Alberdi is a close friend of my husband's," said Kitty promptly, "so of course he's been staying with us during his holiday in England. Last night he and I went up to Town for the evening, and had supper there. By that time the fog was pretty thick, and we were hours getting home. We had a quick nightcap, and then I went to bed, leaving him in the lounge. Should I say, 'leaving him in the lounge with the brandy'?"

Kendrick nodded, and she continued. "This morning at—at seven-thirty? Right. This morning at seven-thirty I went to call him, and found that his bed hadn't been slept in. He wasn't asleep in the lounge either, and I couldn't think where he might be. Then I remembered how interested he'd been in my husband's carpentry, so I went to the basement and—and there he was. He must have fallen down the stair and—"

She paused as Kendrick held up a silencing hand. He strained his ears for a moment, and mouthed, "I thought I heard a footstep in the passage."

Kitty looked at him in some surprise, then shrugged. "I thought I heard a footstep in the passage," she repeated obediently. Kendrick looked at her in despair, but the damage was done.

"I'm afraid you did, Mrs. Olsen," said a voice that struck the journalist as familiar. Mrs. Olsen jumped, and looked panic-stricken. "Will you both please come up with your hands on your heads. I have a gun trained on the stair opening, and the house is surrounded, so you haven't a hope of escape. Come up, please. The lady first, by the way, or I'll shoot on sight."

ELEVEN

For a moment Kendrick hesitated; then he drew the *Cabrito* and nodded to Kitty to go up the stair. With obvious reluctance she did so, and when she reached the top the voice said, "A couple of paces this way, please, Mrs. Olsen. That's fine. Now, if your partner feels like shooting it out with me, we'll no doubt both hit *you* . . . Come on, man! Up!"

Kendrick gave a four-lettered murmur, pocketed the gun and went up with his hands on his head. In the kitchen doorway, holding a pearl-handled Colt .38, stood Bill Hadley.

When he saw Kendrick his jaw dropped and a look of sheer amazement appeared on his face. "Well, blow me down!" he said. "Not even gyved!"

"Huh?" said Kendrick, genuinely puzzled.

"I come galloping over the drawbridge on my snow-white charger," said Hadley, "to rescue my old shipmate from durance vile; and what do I find? I find him dallying in the dungeon with the lady of the manor, and no sign of Alberdi at all."

"Alberdi's out someplace," said Kendrick. Taken colloquially, this was quite true. "I don't know why you thought I required rescuing, but if you're really here with friendly intent, could you stop brandishing that cannon?"

Hadley looked at his gun as if he had never seen it before. "Sorry," he said, and slipped it into a shoulder holster.

"And could we go somewhere less draughty than this passage?" Kitty suggested. "Don, you haven't introduced Sir Lancelot yet." Her self-possession seemed to be hitting on all six again, Kendrick noted with approval. He made the introduction, and the three headed for the lounge.

"The house isn't really surrounded, is it, Mr. Hadley?" asked Kitty as they went.

Hadley gave a deprecating smile. "Only by mist," he admitted. "That was what's called a stratagem."

"And what are you called? A private detective?"

"Not really, no. Let's just say I'm an unconventional fellow who can't keep his nose out of other people's business."

"What made you think I was a prisoner here, Hadley?" said Kendrick when they were all seated. He tried hard to keep the suspicion out of his voice.

"It was a natural inference that you were a prisoner somewhere, and as I knew that Alberdi was staying here—"

"But why should I be a prisoner anywhere?"

Hadley regarded him with mild surprise. "Most kidnapped people are kept prisoner, old boy," he said, "and according to the morning papers you were kidnapped last night."

Kendrick, knowing that there was nobody likely even to have noticed his absence from home yet, far less to have reported him kidnapped, said, "I'm afraid I don't believe you."

"I can't help that," said Hadley. "If it's not true don't blame me, blame the *Courier*. They say you were snatched from a mews near Smith Street, and Scotland Yard questioned the residents, and—"

"Scotland Yard?" said Kendrick and Kitty Olsen, in unison and dismay. Hadley regarded them quizzically.

"A Detective Chief-Inspector, no less," he said. "If you weren't kidnapped, old boy, I suggest you think up some reason why the police found your Super Snipe abandoned in Fulham."

"And why you then found me in the Olsen home in Datchet?"

"Oh, that!" said Hadley, shrugging. "Nobody need ever know I found you anywhere, and frankly I'd as soon nobody did. Let's face it, if I'd rung the door-bell it would be different, but

I couldn't resist the larder window, which means that Mrs. Olsen can charge me with armed housebreaking if she feels like it."

"I don't," said Mrs. Olsen, dimpling.

"That's nice of you. So I'll simply apologize for intruding, and push off. Want a lift to Town, old boy, or—"

"Yes, please," said Kendrick; and then, to Kitty, "You won't forget the story we agreed on, honey?"

Somewhat taken aback, she glanced at the amused Hadley, then looked reproachfully at Kendrick. "No, of course not," she said.

The journalist turned to Hadley and said, "Sound like a guilty couple, don't we? We're not, but Dick Olsen's so unreasonably jealous that if he ever knew I'd been here in his absence . . . Oh, well. Ready for the road when you are."

The morning was chill and damp, but the mist was thinning as the sun rose, and Kendrick saw that they were in a quiet area of self-contained houses with pleasant gardens. Hadley, leading the way to where he had left his car, said, "Whatever story you two agreed on, I'll bet it does the trick."

"How so?"

"Well, dash it! Scripted by a top-flight columnist, delivered by TV's Actress of the Year for nineteen-whatever-it-was . . ."

Kendrick looked at him in surprise. "What's this about the Actress of the Year?" he asked.

"You mean you didn't know she was Kathryn Blane?"

"Who's Kathryn Blane?"

It was Hadley's turn to look surprised. "My dear chap!" he said. "Even if you don't remember her St. Joan, surely you remember the trial. It was . . . can't have been more than six or seven years ago."

"I was still in Canada then."

"Ah! Well, it's a simple enough story. Her husband caught her with one of her boy friends and got killed in the process. It looked open-and-shut till they put her in the witness-box, but then she gave the performance of her life, and somehow or other—I suppose the all-male jury helped—saved her pretty neck. One or two of her less orthodox practices had come to light, though, and her career was over. She sold her memoirs to a Sunday paper, of course, but after that I imagine she was glad to marry Olsen and fade from sight. This is the old bus." He halted beside a gleaming blue Cresta saloon.

As Kendrick climbed into the front passenger seat he reflected wryly on his "generous gesture" to the terrified child. Just who, he wondered, had been kidding whom?

Hadley switched on the inside light, took a folded newspaper from the glove compartment and said, "There you are, old boy. Read it for yourself."

It was the 3 a.m. edition of the *Daily Courier,* and as Kendrick read the story he realized that Lynn had been right, and the "witch across the way" had indeed been at her observation post. There was no mention of Lynn by name—she was merely "a friend he had been visiting"—but there was an interview with Miss Emma Sankey, and he formed the impression (correctly) that it was that lady who had telephoned the story to the paper.

The newsroom had evidently checked with Scotland Yard and been told of the finding of Kendrick's car. A Yard spokesman had declined to confirm the incident as an abduction— the comings and goings of Fleet Street columnists, he had indicated, were often mysterious—but he had clearly been unable to explain why it took Detective Chief-Inspector Dane of the Special Branch to investigate it. The *Courier* concluded by describing the functions of the Branch, mentioned that Kendrick had just returned from South America, and left it at that; a breakfast-table titbit for two million homes.

"The spokesman was right, of course," said Kendrick, handing back the paper. "In my job, Hadley, you make some pretty odd acquaintances. That guy in my car was a shy ex-convict with a story to sell. We drove to Fulham, where I checked some of his facts, and then we transferred to a less conspicuous vehicle to drive half over the Home Counties checking the remainder. Came the dawn, and with it the *Courier* story. Any questions?"

"No. It's very ingenious."

"You mean you don't believe it?"

"Of course I don't. I think the man in your car was Alberdi, and he stuck a gun in your back and—"

"Why Alberdi?"

"He tailed you from Euston to your flat on Saturday morning, called on you, and left hurriedly, looking very unhappy. At least, so I'm informed by a colleague, who then followed him and Mrs. Olsen out to Datchet. So when I read that you'd been snatched and the Special Branch was interested, I thought there was a very good chance that Alberdi had decided to have another interview with you, but on his home ground for a change. I believe you transferred to another car in Fulham, all right, but I think Mrs. Olsen was driving it. Some time between then and my arrival on the scene she obviously double-crossed Alberdi and teamed up with you; which is a pity, for it ruined my rescue act. I had counted on putting you under an obligation to me."

"Why?"

"Let's discuss that over bacon and eggs," said Hadley. "I don't know about you, but I'm starving."

They drove through Langley and followed the busy A4 eastwards till they came to a pull-up called, with engaging simplicity, Mo's. Here, when they had carried their plates to a table that offered reasonable privacy for conversation, Kendrick said, "Right. Who are you, what are you, and what's your angle?"

Hadley hesitated. "No," he said. "First I'll have to ask you to promise not to print anything I may tell you, unless and until I specifically give you permission."

"Okay—provided it isn't something I know already."

"That's fair enough, so I'll answer your questions. I'm William Arbuthnot Hadley, I'm a career diplomat currently doing a stretch at Headquarters, and I'm engaged in trying to prevent something that might jeopardize this country's happy relations with the Republic of Colombia."

"And why did you want to put me under an obligation?"

"Because I think you could help me in what I'm trying to do. I imagine you've heard of a rebel called Colonel Carlos Urquiza?"

"I have."

"When his insurrection was squashed he disappeared. It's virtually certain that some Britishers in Barranquilla helped him, that somehow or other they smuggled him into England, and that he's still here."

"Unbeknownst to the authorities? Or winked at?"

"Entirely unbeknownst. If the F.O. had been able to locate him he'd have been pushed out pronto. Colombia still wants to bring the blighter to trial, and if he ever shows up anywhere they'll undoubtedly try to extradite him. We don't give a damn about that, so long as it isn't British soil he shows up on. If it is, then neither Colombia nor anybody else will believe he's been living here without tacit official permission; and relations will, to put it mildly, deteriorate."

"Even if it's the British authorities who find him and promptly deport him?"

"That would have been all right if it had happened immediately he got here, old boy, but now it's two years too late. Now they'd say we were afraid he was about to be found by somebody else, and we'd thrown him to the wolves to save our national face."

"They probably would, at that," Kendrick agreed. "So?"

"So this is where I come in, and it's a very welcome change

from monitoring Spanish broadcasts, I can assure you. Er—
Kendrick, do you happen to know the Manuela Gomez background at all?"

"Sure. Under the affectionate pet-name of The Rattlesnake,
she was one of the Colonel's most active supporters. Under her
real name of Señora Belgrano she's the widow of his right-
hand man."

"True, as far as it goes. But the Belgrano marriage was . . .
shall we say, more honoured in the breach than the observance;
by both partners. Boys' clubs were his hobby. And for years
Manuela was—and no doubt by now again is—the Colonel's
querida. Lady friend, as we call it in genteel circles."

Kendrick whistled softly. "You think she's come over here
to join him?"

"We're convinced of it. They both probably think the heat's
off by this time. Anyway, when she applied for a British visa
she was given one, and I was flown out to Montreal to make
the crossing with her and try to get our long-awaited lead."

"Well, well!" said Kendrick. "And I never even guessed that
your interest in her was purely professional. Brother, can you
dissemble!"

The diplomat gave a rather shame-faced grin. "I cannot deny
that I was happy in my work," he said, "at least until Wednesday, when I over-estimated my manly appeal. I wanted to
search her cabin for any kind of line on Urquiza's whereabouts, but I couldn't risk being caught there and rousing her
suspicions, so I decided I'd have to be invited in and then dope
her drink or something."

"Instead of which, she slapped your wrist?"

"It wasn't my wrist," said Hadley feelingly. "Believe me, the
'rattlesnake' tag didn't get tied to her by accident. Anyway,
that was that. She didn't invite me in, so I retired from the fray
and decided simply to tail her. But somehow or other she gave
both myself and a shore-based colleague the slip at Greenock,

so I concentrated on you instead, because my contact in the Purser's Bureau had told me the two of you were booked in at the St. Enoch. There, of course, I found that she'd slipped you too, but I doubted if she'd done it as gladly as she'd slipped me. I thought she might phone you at the hotel, so I tried to latch onto you for the evening; but you weren't having any. I suspect that your mood was much the same as mine had been on Wednesday night." He looked at his watch, and said, "Must be on my way. We can finish our talk in the car."

The Cresta nosed out into the traffic again, and for a time the diplomat was too busy driving to talk. When conditions eased slightly he said, "Look, it's really no concern of mine, I suppose, but—this business of Dane investigating your disappearance—you're not by any chance working on something for the Special Branch, are you?"

"Heck, no!" said Kendrick. "Far from it."

"Good. As you seem to have tangled with a bunch of Reds I was afraid you might be, and the less I see and hear of the Special Branch at present, the happier I'll be."

"Really? I thought you co-operated with them pretty closely."

"Oh, we do—when we can. But the police are a law-abiding lot, old boy, and if they got on the Urquiza trail it could be disastrous. If they found him they'd arrest him, he'd appear in court charged with illegal entry, the news would flash round the globe, and bang would go our beautiful friendship with Colombia."

"Whereas if it's the F.O. that finds him?"

"I fancy he'll be given forged papers, if he hasn't already got some, a one-way ticket to Madrid or somewhere, and very clear orders not to come back. One thing I do know is that there won't be any publicity."

Kendrick chuckled. "You've chosen a strange confidant, Hadley," he said.

"I didn't choose you, old boy, you were thrust on me by a

malign fate; and if my chief even guessed that I was trying to make an ally of you he'd spontaneously combust. He'd as soon trust a cobra as a columnist any day. But I think you could help me to find Urquiza, and that's why I hoped to spring you from your captivity. One good turn deserves another, as they say, so I hoped that perhaps you'd help even though you couldn't possibly get a story out of it."

Kendrick was silent for a time, as they crawled through the Brentford traffic.

Then he said, "If I did decide to sacrifice a story for sheer love of the Mother Country, what would you want me to do?"

"Interview a fortune-teller," said Hadley, promptly and hopefully. "We're pretty sure she acts as a kind of private post office for Urquiza—you know, that his adherents, both in Colombia and in exile, route their correspondence with him through her. Not being cops, unfortunately, we can't pull her in and grill her. And simply keeping an eye on her isn't the slightest use."

"Why not?"

"My dear chap! Fortune-tellers have the greatest variety of clients on earth—no barriers of class, race, age or sex. Moreover, each one is dealt with in private. How is an outside observer to guess which of fifty assorted customers is the one with the secret despatch in his hollow tooth?"

Kendrick considered this, and saw the truth of it. As a clearing-house for clandestine correspondence, a fortune-teller's salon would take a lot of beating. Not even doctors or bar-tenders had more diversified clienteles. What he did not see, however, was how his interviewing her would help. He said so.

"Dash it," said Hadley, "she'd fall over herself to tell you things, and probably let you sit behind a curtain or somewhere to overhear her in action. These people thrive on publicity, and the prospect of a write-up by Don Kendrick of the *Bulletin* . . ."

Kendrick regarded him ironically, and said, "You think she'd tell me all about her work for Urquiza? Or do you merely hope that I might be lucky enough to see a client pull a roll of micro-film out of his false beard?"

Hadley gave him a pained look and said, "Really, old boy! No, but I do think that a trained interviewer like yourself, with no limit to the number or nature of the topics he could bring up, might very well dig up some little detail that would give us a lead. And there's another reason, of course, why you're the only man for the job."

"What's that?"

"You know Manuela, and if she happened to show up around the fairground, I'm pretty sure you'd recognize her; even with a blonde wig and dark glasses or what-have-you."

"Yes," said Kendrick absently, "I guess that's right." He was reflecting that the plan contained a hole you could drive a truck through; and he was quite sure that William Arbuthnot Hadley knew it.

If an inquisitive columnist, already involved with Manuela and her dangerous despatches, suddenly turned up asking questions at the private post office, it would be "Panic Stations All Hands" for Urquiza and his friends. And that, most probably, was just what Hadley hoped for: a scare that might flush the Colonel out of his nest and give the F.O. a chance to shoo him aboard the plane for Spain.

Then why wasn't Hadley being frank about his purpose? The answer, no doubt, was that he shared Lynn Everett's views on the "English tie-up with Colombian politics" into which she had advised Kendrick not to pry. "I like you better without a knife in your back," she had said.

Hadley, presumably, didn't care if Kendrick got a full set of chef's carving-irons in his back, provided the quarry broke cover; but the diplomat was afraid Kendrick wouldn't touch the job if he knew it might prove dangerous. Hence the specious sales-talk. Well, one good turn certainly deserves another; but so does one doublecross.

"Okay, Hadley," he said. "I'll interview your fairground fortune-teller; and we'll see where it gets us."

TWELVE

Hadley dropped him at Victoria Station, giving him one of the fortune-teller's advertising leaflets, and also a Piccadilly telephone number at which he, Hadley, could be contacted without any risk of his anti-columnar chief's learning that he had enlisted the aid of a cobra. "It's my flat, old boy," he explained. "If I'm not there myself, you can safely leave a message with my . . . kid sister." He grinned, waved, and drove off into a traffic jam.

Madame Zingara, the leaflet read, *Consultant to Royalty. Clairvoyance. Cartomancy. Palmistry. Crystal-gazing.* Below a grisly representation of the human hand an address had been rubber-stamped, slightly askew: *The Pleasure Dome, Bexhill-on-Sea, Sussex.*

Kendrick pocketed the leaflet, found a vacant phone-box in the station, and rang Lynn's office. Her assessment of William A. Hadley, he felt, might be helpful.

The voice that answered her extension, however, was male, and informed him that Miss Everett was on compassionate leave. Kendrick expressed concern, and trusted that there was nothing seriously wrong. "Some family illness, I am told," said the man huffily. "A parent, I presume, but I'm afraid I have no details. Apparently her application went straight to the Director." Then, evidently realizing that injured dignity had made him say too much, he added a brisk "Good morning," and hung up.

Kendrick was smiling as he left the box and headed for the washroom and barber's shop. He had never met Lynn's parents, but he had met her Director, and he knew that that august official was also her godfather and indulgent honorary uncle. Lynn had more than once wheedled brief absences out of him for reasons other than those that went into the record, and it sounded as if she had done so again. Whatever the little redhead might be up to, Kendrick was prepared to bet that she wasn't within a hundred miles of a parental sickbed.

As he freshened himself he considered all that he had learned in the past few hours. Adding Hadley's contribution onto Kitty Olsen's, and viewing both in the light of what Lynn had told him previously, he began to see a picture emerge. It was a faceless picture—apart from John Doe—of British business men, with some stake in Colombia, befriending Urquiza for their own commercial ends; hiding him in England while he and his devoted *norteños* back home planned a second rising, this time with surreptitious British money behind it; and finally fetching Manuela over to . . . to do what?

Submit the battle-plan to Doe & Co. for financial approval? Bring her specialized persuasion to bear on the Colonel if, as was quite possible, an easy life in exile had lessened his urge to risk the firing-squad once more? The reason didn't really matter very much. Any way you looked at it, the set-up was page one dynamite.

Feeling moderately clean again, he returned to the row of telephone-boxes, found Richard Olsen's number in the appropriate directory, and called it. Kitty answered and, when he had identified himself and asked to speak to Primo, told him that Mr. Alberdi had had an accident and was now in hospital. Her tone was guarded, and Kendrick guessed that she was afraid the line was being tapped. Considering her husband's political colouration, he felt, she might be right at that. He expressed shocked surprise, and she gave him details. "Apparently he fractured his skull," she ended, "and got compression of the brain. They operated right away, though, and they say his condition is satisfactory. So far."

Kendrick sent his best wishes for a speedy recovery, and was perfectly sincere in doing so. Then he looked at his watch, and decided that he could not stall the police much longer.

He phoned the *Post*, the evening sister of his own paper, and briefed it to pour patronizing scorn on the *Courier*'s kidnapping story; then asked if the Clancy inquest verdict was yet to hand. No, they told him, it was not. Sadly, he rang Scotland Yard, and asked for Chief-Inspector Dane.

"Don Kendrick here," he said, trying to sound aggrieved. "Dane, who gave that cock-and-bull yarn about me to the *Courier?* And where's my car?"

Twenty minutes later, in the detective's office, he told the "shy ex-convict" tale that he had already tried out on Hadley and given, in amplified form, to the *Post*. Dane listened impassively, then nodded.

"Well, well!" he said. "A false alarm, eh? Kendrick, before we go any further, I ought to tell you that Joe Clancy had fairly advanced heart disease, and that that's what killed him. They may be able to prosecute you under the Litter Act or something, but not for murder. So now that that's off your mind perhaps you'll be readier to co-operate. Have you been home since yesterday?"

Trying not to let his relief be too obvious, Kendrick shook his head; and then attempted to look not only angry, which he was, but also surprised, which he was not, when Dane told him what had happened to his flat. "Any idea who might have been responsible?" the detective asked.

"I've a darned strong suspicion. I should think it was almost certainly that Latin lunatic you say Howard the porter told you about. For some reason he thought, quite mistakenly, that I knew the whereabouts of some documents he wanted. He swore blind that his wife had given them to me to smuggle ashore for her from the *Duchess of Malfi*, and he started to play rough when I told him I knew nothing about them. That's how the bullet you found came to get into the woodwork."

Dane's lips twitched, and he said, "Also, I take it, how the lady in the flat below came to hear a heavy crash?"

"Yes. I knocked him out, but he woke up and escaped while I was talking to Howard on the blower."

"Why on earth didn't you call the police, Kendrick?"

Kendrick gave him an expressive look. "Let's just say it wasn't my day for calling the police, shall we?" he suggested. "I was fresh off that overnight train, remember."

"And you really hadn't smuggled anything ashore for Mrs. Gomez?"

"She hadn't even asked me to," said Kendrick truthfully, and then remembered that Dane had examined his apartment and had therefore undoubtedly noticed the tell-tale care with which certain stitching had been unpicked. "And if you're about to enquire," he added, "what I hid in the lining of my tux, I'll decline to reply on the grounds that the answer might incriminate me. I won't even admit that it was contraband. But I will give you my word that I didn't put it there at the request of Mrs. Gomez."

Dane eyed him speculatively for a time, then said, "I take it you don't know where this fellow Gomez is now?"

"I don't," said Kendrick, grateful that Kitty Olsen had not given him the name of the hospital.

"And Manuela Gomez? The Webster Line couldn't give us her English address."

"Nor can I, I'm afraid. She never mentioned it to me."

"Reverting to these documents Gomez wanted—did he explain what they were?"

"No. He simply called them 'the papers Manuela gave you', and as she hadn't given me any papers I didn't bother asking him what they were supposed to be."

"Do you think they're what Clancy was looking for when you caught him in your sleeping compartment?"

Kendrick surveyed the detective thoughtfully for a moment.

"Tell me," he said, "what's the maximum penalty for offences under the Litter Act?"

Dane laughed. "Search me," he said. "But you were seen waltzing the corpse down the corridor, so there's not much point in denying it."

"Well," said the journalist, "in the light of later events, I suppose he must have been hoping to find the papers. At the time, of course, I couldn't think what he'd been after, for I hadn't heard of them then."

"If you weren't already mixed up in the affair somehow, Kendrick, what the devil made you dump the body instead of reporting it?"

"Sheer panic, I think," said Kendrick honestly. "Don't forget that only a few hours earlier Captain Nicholson had been congratulating me on getting away with the murder of Frank Farrell. I figured that a man can have too many coincidences in his life."

"You know, I believe that could be true," said Dane, nodding. "Right, then. If you'll just give us your fingerprints for elimination purposes, I fancy that'll be all for the present. I don't think for one moment that you've told me the whole truth today, but apart from the nonsense about the ex-convict I don't think you've told me any downright lies either; and that's a step in the right direction. Next time I'll just have to try and ask better questions."

Kendrick collected his car and drove to Chelsea. There had been an odd omission from Dane's questioning, and he wondered why. If Howard had told the detective about Gomez, it was a certainty that he had also mentioned the second visitor, the more so as Kendrick had arranged to have the man shadowed when he left. Yet Dane had not once referred to him. Curious.

The fog had cleared hours before, and the sun shone from a blue sky; but his car radio informed him that misty conditions were expected to return in the evening. If he was going down to

Bexhill-on-Sea by road, he thought, to interview Madame Zingara, he had better leave as early as possible. He could, of
course, go by train. Or maybe it would be more intelligent to
go to bed, and postpone the trip till next day. He was becoming
increasingly conscious that he had spent yet one more sleepless
night.

The sight of his apartment did nothing to revive him. Two
cleaners had toiled on it all morning, tidying up the worst of
the mess, but it still looked pretty bad. He would have hours of
work to do, sorting out his papers and repairing his books and
pictures, but he was in no mood to start. He was in no mood,
either, to seek repose in a bed whose mattress had been hacked
to pieces. He threw a few clothes into a grip, and was on the
point of leaving when the manager of the block appeared with
an insurance inspector.

They were there to examine the furniture, but as Kendrick's
own possessions were insured with the same firm he decided to
stay and arrange about his personal claims. It was mid-after-
noon before he was free, and by then he had decided on his
course of action. All roads, it seemed, led to Sussex, so he
would kill three birds with one tank-full of Shell.

He would first call at the vehicle licencing office in the county
town of Lewes, and get the name and address that went with
the number-plate TPN 2385. He would then drive on to
Brighton and leave Manuela's despatch with old Markham for
deciphering. Finally he would go to Bexhill, take a room with
unmutilated bed in some quiet hotel there, and chalk up at
least twelve hours of sack time before he tackled the fortune-
teller.

He had promised to let Hadley know in advance when he intended to interview her, so he now rang the Piccadilly number
and left a message. The diplomat's "kid sister," he was
amused to find, had a delicious but very far from English accent.

Then he drove to the Sloane Square post office and asked the

Callers' Letters clerk for the mail for Donald Kendrick. She looked at him rather oddly, and he guessed that she had read the kidnapping story but not the *Post*'s contradiction of it. "I'm afraid there isn't any," she said, after making a show of searching the "K" pigeonhole.

"But there has to be," said Kendrick, and displayed his driving-licence by way of identifying himself. "A manila envelope, mailed in the King's Road Saturday."

The girl inspected the licence, and a worried look crept into her eyes. "Mr. Kendrick, I—I'm afraid there's been some mistake," she said. "Another man collected that letter hours ago."

Kendrick stared at her unbelievingly. "Another man?" he echoed. "But—surely you asked him for identification?"

"Of course I did, and he gave me this." She reached under the counter, and handed him one of his own business cards. "So I gave him the letter. It was only when I heard you speak just now that I suddenly remembered being told once that Don Kendrick of the *Bulletin* was a young Canadian."

The girl looked stricken, but no more so than Kendrick. "Whereas this guy was a middle-aged Englishman, I take it?" he said bleakly. He was recalling John Doe's very last words to him: *the little drawer in your desk, beside your business cards.* It did not need the clerk's description to tell him who now had the ciphered battle-plans.

Indiscriminately cursing John Doe, the clerk, the traffic and his own stupidity, Kendrick sent the Super Snipe down Lower Sloane Street at an angry and illegal speed. He crossed the river by Chelsea Bridge and, keeping to the quieter streets as much as possible, threaded a way through South London.

It was easy enough, with hindsight, to see where he had gone wrong. He ought never to have told John Doe that the letter was temporarily out of his possession, but perfectly safe until wanted. Heck, the words practically implied that it was in the mail—particularly to a man who, watching the block until Kendrick should leave his flat empty, had most likely seen him drop something in the mailbox as he went out! What a master of intrigue he had turned out to be!

The envelope might, of course, have been addressed to the *Bulletin* Office or back to Castlemaine Court, or even to some friend. But Doe, having prudently pocketed some of the journalist's cards when he came on them, and having nothing to lose but his time, had no doubt gone round all the near-by post offices on spec—and come up with the winning ticket.

Visualizing the smile of triumph on the man's face, Kendrick went through the end of an amber light, shaved the front bumper of a quick-starting MG, and realized that if he wanted to reach Sussex in one piece he had better cool down and do some driving.

At Purley he joined the A22, and made fair speed through Surrey to the county border. East Grinstead slowed him down, but at Wych Cross he forked right onto A275, and had a clear run through to Lewes. He located the vehicle licencing office minutes before it closed.

He might have saved himself the trouble; for it is the law of the land that those who seek information about registered car-owners must satisfy the authorities that they have reasonable cause for requiring same. And, for the first time in his journalistic career, he met an official who apparently abode by the letter of that law. Neither the magic name of the *Bulletin* nor the broad hint of a bribe could budge him, and even when Kendrick invented plausible details of a suspected hit-and-run he still shook his head.

"Sorry, sir," he said. "I'd have to refer that to higher authority." Then, seeing the Canadian's expression, he added, "Look, Mr. Kendrick, maybe I ought not to tell you this, but I don't want you to think I'm just a bloody-minded bureaucrat. Scotland Yard were on, soon as we opened this morning, also asking who owned that number. And they particularly warned us that they didn't want the party concerned to know they'd been enquiring."

"Did they forbid you to give the information to anyone else who might ask?"

"Not in so many words, sir, but they made it quite clear that they didn't want this chap to be alerted in any way. And if you don't mind my saying so, giving his name and address to a newspaper man wouldn't be the best way of keeping things quiet."

Kendrick looked at him hopelessly. "I guess you're right," he said. "Anyhow, thanks for tipping me off about the Yard."

He returned to his car and sat in the driving-seat for a while without switching on the ignition. At least he now knew why Tony Dane had not bothered to ask him about John Doe. The Yard had by that time known more about the gentleman than Kendrick did. Howard must have told Dane of the tailing job; then Alf Groves the cab-driver, questioned in turn, had given them the car-number; Dane, or whoever did the phoning, had effectively buttoned the registration clerk's mouth. And that was that.

Coming right on top of the loss of the battle-plans, it was a pretty sickening blow. Madame Zingara was now his only remaining lead, and at the moment she looked a rather unpromising one. Still, he supposed he had better push on to Bexhill.

The accumulated weariness of days pressed on him as he drove eastwards, and more than once he almost dozed off. *Bexhill or bust!* he told himself firmly, and rolled down the windows to see if fresh air would help. There was more than a hint of mist in it, mist that would probably grow thicker as he got nearer the sea. He yawned hugely, corrected a swerve, and pulled himself together. Maybe the radio would keep him awake.

The radio, however, seemed to have a jinx on it, for no matter where he went on the dial he could get only one station, its signal apparently strong enough to drown all competition. And the music it was offering was not particularly rousing; a fact explained when the piece ended and a man's voice said, "This is the Morpheus Mattress Hour from Radio Samantha. Are *you* finding it hard to get to sleep these nights?"

"Are you kidding?" said Kendrick sourly, and switched off.

Radio Samantha was a new one, he thought. It must be yet another of the so-called "pirates." He had done an article on these sea-borne stations when they first impinged on England in the shape of Radio Caroline, an Irish-owned ex-ferryboat anchored in international waters off the east coast, beaming music and commercials into the B.B.C.'s commercial-less domain. At that time there had been only two others in Europe —Radio Veronica off the Netherlands and Radio something else off Scandinavia—but now the seas seemed to be crawling with them. He made one last attempt to tune in something else, got nothing but whispers against a waxing and waning background of soporific strings, and resigned himself to silence.

He passed through Polegate and Pevensey, and the mist thickened as the miles fell behind. It couldn't be much farther now, though. What had that last signpost said? Wooden something? No, Cooden, that was it; Cooden Beach. More miles fell behind, and he found that he was driving along a shadowy esplanade, with the sea dimly visible on his right. He pulled up beside the only pedestrian in view, asked where he was, and learned that he had overshot his target by about four miles. The end of a perfect day.

And by hokey! it would be the end too, for he was darned if he was going to drive back and look for the turning he ought to have taken. The lights of an hotel shone diffusely ahead, and at its door he stopped again; kept his drooping eyelids ajar long enough to book a room, get up to it, and undress; and was between the sheets before it struck him that he had not eaten since Mo's.

Before he could decide what to do about it he was asleep.

THIRTEEN

Thirteen hours later he stood at his bedroom window, watching the last wisps of mist disperse above the calm surface of the English Channel, and reflecting that only five days back he had been looking through a porthole at much more turbulent waters. It seemed longer.

He went ravenously downstairs and ordered a gigantic breakfast; most of which, fortunately, he had consumed before he opened the *Daily Courier* and found himself again in the news. *Columnist Denies Abduction Report* was the headline, but it was the accompanying photograph that put him right off his food. *Don Kendrick and a Friend,* it was captioned. It had presumably been taken by one of those freelance menaces who infest the more profitable nightspots, and it showed the columnist at table with a buxom brunette, deeply absorbed in a sidelong study of his companion's *décolletage.* Trust the *Courier* to dig up a dilly like that!

Wincing, he turned to the story, which confirmed what the choice of picture had already suggested—that the *Post*'s "patronizing scorn" had really got under somebody's skin. After a brief recap of what it called "our ridiculous *canard,*" the paper gave Kendrick's own version of the incident, skilfully worded to seem less plausible than ever, and then went on to tell how the columnist's flat had been ransacked by burglars earlier in the day; "apparently as a prelude to his not being kidnapped after all."

The heavy irony continued for another couple of paragraphs, but Kendrick did not read them. He was staring again in fascinated disgust at the picture. If the brunette's parents happened to see it, he thought, there'd be a quick end to one more beautiful friendship. And he could hardly blame them. No doubt the effect was due to some trick of the lighting, but if one did not know that, and if one did not know Kendrick either, one might almost have mistaken his expression for a lecherous leer.

He drove to Bexhill and without difficulty found the Pleasure Dome. It was a vaguely Byzantine structure of considerable size, occupying an island site not far back from the beach, and he drove round it looking for a car-park. There was a small one by the rear entrance, but it was marked *Private—Dome Staff Only,* so he returned to the front, left the Humber by the curb, and went in.

Madame Zingara's booth was just inside the main door, but he passed it with an uninterested glance and strolled on aimlessly. The Dome was spacious and uncrowded. Blaring canned music set the fairground atmosphere if you closed your eyes, but with October only hours away many of the sideshows had closed down. Workmen were dismantling the Space Cruiser, and there were other signs that the season was almost over.

Kendrick played the pin-tables for a time, vainly trying to spot the watcher he felt certain Hadley would have planted, and then went into the shooting gallery.

Originally, when he had made his deal with the diplomat, his scheme had been simple. He had intended to use Manuela's precious letter as a lever for bargaining, and thereby, he had hoped, induce Madame Zingara to open up and give him something he could print without breaking his word to Hadley. The loss of the letter had of course knocked this little double-cross on the head, so he was now contemplating another. His promise bound him to interview the fortune-teller, but he had not guaranteed that it would be a press interview. He now proposed, therefore, to visit her as an ordinary—and anonymous—holidaymaking client. There was no point in inviting a knife in the back unless it seemed likely to show a profit.

The air-guns in the gallery were not designed for accuracy, but after two shillings' worth of sighting shots he got reasonably on target, and won a large red balloon (inflated), a Pebbles doll, and a Union Jack from Japan. With these as holidaymaking camouflage he strolled towards the exit and came to an apparently irresolute halt at the fortune-teller's door.

It promptly opened and a raven-tressed head came round the edge. "You like a consultation, pretty gentleman?" the girl invited, pleasantly combining the Mayfair idiom with the Gypsy. "Madame will be free in one minute." She was an attractive kid, twenty perhaps, with big dark eyes and a promisingly full underlip.

Kendrick smiled, shrugged, and went into a tiny "front office" with black drapes on its inner side. On learning that cartomancy, about which he had been curious ever since reading the advertising leaflet, was simply fortune-telling with playing-cards, he elected to have his palm read, paid his fee, and sat down to wait.

No, said the girl when he asked her, she didn't think Bexhill was the gayest spot on earth, though she had seen worse. No, she had not lived here very long—only since the beginning of the month. Before that? Oh, various places—Eastbourne, Worthing, Bognor—Madame did not like to spend too long in any one town. Yes, the kid supposed they would be moving again shortly. Oh, Brighton, perhaps, or some other all-year-round resort.

No, she was afraid she couldn't go to a movie that night, thank him all the same. When the salon closed she had to drive Madame back to the caravan and make supper; and anyway Madame did not like her to go out with strangers. Yes, she lived with Madame. Madame, as a matter of fact, was her grandmother. Well, no, Zingara wasn't really their name, but . . . Hey! He asked an awful lot of questions, didn't he?

A middle-aged woman came through the drapes and, as she went out of the door, Kendrick said, "Me now?"

The girl nodded, rising. "I'll just find out if Madame is ready." She slipped through the curtains and he heard the murmur of voices, though he could not distinguish the words. In a minute she reappeared and held the drapes open for him.

He found himself in a greenish gloom that smelt of incense. The fortune-teller, a shapeless figure in a loose black robe and a black lace mantilla, was seated behind a table with a black velvet cloth and an unlit desk-lamp on it. A bony hand waved him to the client's chair in front of the table, and he sat down.

"Please, your left hand first. That tells the character." The voice, hoarse and low-pitched, suggested a lifelong devotion to whisky, but was somehow none the less impressive for that. Kendrick laid his hand on the table, the desk-lamp clicked on, and the palmist said, "You were born many miles from this country."

Kendrick refrained from pointing out that most people with his kind of accent had been, and said, "Yes."

"You no longer live in your native land, however. You adopted England some years ago."

That was better, he thought. Either the old girl—or, more probably, her sharp-eyed granddaughter—had noticed that his lounge suit, by no means new, was London-tailored. "Yes," he said again.

"You are a restless, independent person. You are unmarried. You are fond of your work—it is creative work, I think, not routine; writing of some kind, perhaps. But you are fond of pleasure also, perhaps too fond of it. You are particularly fond of women."

Was that really graven on his palm, Kendrick wondered, or merely a deduction from his attempt to date the granddaughter? He had no doubt that the kid briefed Madame as best she could before showing in a client. "You think so, huh?" he said.

"I can read it here," said the palmist, and went on to read a number of more flattering traits such as truthfulness, courage, loyalty, initiative and integrity. Kendrick disclaimed none of them. He was beginning to enjoy himself.

"And now, please, the right hand."

"What does the right hand tell?" asked the journalist as he made the exchange.

"Fortune . . . This is strange. So often we say, 'You will make a long journey across water,' that people have come to think it is a joke, but . . ."

"I'm going to make one all the same?"

"Either that or you have just made it. A double journey. Yes, I think that is it. I think you have revisited the western world recently, and have only just returned. Yes?"

"On the button," said Kendrick. How the heck had she got that one?

Then the obvious explanation struck him. She knew who he was, of course. Either she or the girl had recognized him from the *Courier* photograph—which incidentally gave ample grounds for guessing that he was unmarried but liked women—and had remembered the paper's previous story, with its reference to his recent return from South America. The old dame might even have heard of him from Manuela, come to think of it. "How about the future?" he asked. That should fix her.

There was a long silence while the glittering eyes studied his palm, and he speculated idly on the present whereabouts of the glamorous widow Gomez. "You will marry," the hoarse voice croaked at last, "but not soon. And the woman you will wed is not the one you are thinking about at this moment."

Slightly startled—she couldn't be a mind-reader too, could she?—Kendrick could only say, "She's not, huh?"

"No. Your bride will be small and fair. The other is tall and dark and . . . she is very well figured."

"She sure is," Kendrick agreed. If Madame Zingara wanted to talk about Manuela, that was okay with him.

"But your ways will soon part—may already have parted; I

am not certain. Perhaps she is more interested in her career. She is . . . a model, I think, or an actress. Perhaps both?"

What was La Zingara trying to do, confuse the issue? He shook his head, and could not resist saying, "No—only 'a very unimportant *costurera*'."

The effect was startling. The palmist sat up as if galvanized, and said sharply, "You speak Spanish?"

"Not I. I was quoting the girl. She said it meant sempstress."

Across the cone of light the small eyes stared at him almost accusingly, then dropped again to his palm. "The woman you marry . . ." The tired, whisky-tone was back again, and the rest of the "consultation" was routine.

When it was over he rose and said, "Thank you, Madame Zingara. Extremely interesting."

"I do my best . . . Will you please ask Inez to come in?"

Rightly guessing that Inez was the girl, Kendrick did so, and then left, feeling distinctly puzzled. Why had his use of a Spanish word so startled the old gal, when she knew he was fresh back from South America? Darn it, she had been describing Manuela, and—it suddenly hit him that she had probably not been describing Manuela at all. She had almost certainly been describing the brunette in the *Courier* picture; who was in fact an ambitious young model and bit-player, and whom indeed the palmist might well have seen on TV or in fashion ads.

The more he thought about it, the more likely this seemed. Right up until he said *costurera*, then, Madame Zingara— misled, perhaps, by his holidaymaking camouflage—must have believed that he had wandered into her salon by sheer chance. When he did say it, of course, she had realized that he was talking about Manuela, had probably thought he was saying, in effect, "I know you're one of the Urquiza mob." It looked as if, in spite of himself, he might have achieved the result Bill Hadley wanted.

He saw a very small girl gazing covetously at his Pebbles

doll, and seized the opportunity to get rid of it and the other prizes. Brushing aside the mother's thanks—"Honest, ma'am, I don't play with that kind of dolly myself"—he found a position from which he could unobtrusively watch the fortune-teller's door. It could be, of course, that nothing would happen; but he was pretty sure they had no telephone in the booth, so if Madame Zingara did feel like sending out a "Panic Stations" call . . .

Five minutes passed, and then the door opened and Inez looked out. Kendrick slid behind a pillar, and apparently the girl's eyes missed him, for she said something over her shoulder and hung a "Closed" card on the door-handle. She was then joined by a figure that, for a moment, Kendrick did not recognize. Seen in daylight, with a nondescript hat and a drab coat replacing mantilla and robe, the "Consultant to Royalty" looked like a very ordinary suburban housewife—albeit from the suburbs of Naples or Barcelona rather than Bexhill.

The two walked quickly through the Dome towards the rear exit, so Kendrick went out to the Super Snipe, waited for a few seconds, and then drove slowly round to the back of the building. His timing was excellent. A jeep was coming out of the staff car-park, Inez at the wheel, the palmist hunched up by her side. He gave them a reasonable lead and then followed.

The route lay inland and soon took them clear of the town. There were quiet roads lined with bungalows, and then a mile stretch, mainly climbing, between fields with cattle in them. As he topped the crest he saw a caravan-site two hundred yards downhill, and promptly stopped. If this was not journey's end he could easily catch up, but if it was he did not want to go too near.

It was. The jeep pulled up at the entrance, and the pair walked across the asphalt to a very stylish trailer in daffodil yellow slashed with lilac. The site, Kendrick thought, would probably hold about forty caravans at the height of the season, but now there was a bare dozen, spaced sufficiently far apart to give their inhabitants at least the illusion of some privacy.

On the steps of the trailer nearest the Zingara one a man sat smoking, and something familiar in the set of the shoulders made Kendrick reach for his binoculars. Yes, it was Bill Hadley all right. He saw the Englishman rise, flick away his cigarette-butt and go inside, closing the door.

For some minutes nothing happened, and then Inez appeared. She strode back to the jeep and, as she drove off, Kendrick followed. A couple of right-angled turns brought them out on an A-class road, and they headed east. Bulverhythe and St. Leonards fell behind, and then they were in the little town of Hastings, where modern history began. Kendrick thought of that fateful October D-Day nine centuries before, and grinned at a poster on the pier approach. *See Sussex as the Normans Never Did, with King Harold Helicopters Limited.*

Beyond the town they followed a quiet, undulating road between trees. Five miles later the jeep stopped abruptly, just short of a T-junction; and Kendrick, who had allowed himself to get too close, could only drive past and hope the girl would not recognize him. Round the first bend he stopped, took his binoculars, and walked back till he could see the jeep. If anyone came along he was bird-watching.

Inez was reading something, and frowning at it. Then she looked up, straight at him, and instinctively he ducked back, though at that distance she was unlikely to have noticed him. When he risked another peep she was licking and sealing an envelope. She pocketed it, threw some small object out of the car, made a right-handed turn and accelerated up the side-road.

By the time Kendrick got back to the T-junction the jeep was out of sight, but he pulled up and searched the ditch until he found what must be the thing the girl had thrown out. As he had expected, it was a torn and crumpled envelope; and, as he had feared, it was empty and unaddressed.

The explanation, he thought as he drove up the side-road, was not hard to guess. Inez, entrusted with a letter to deliver, but not with a knowledge of its contents, had brought along a spare envelope and repaired the omission; which suggested that, if she knew about the Urquiza set-up at all, she certainly had not been told of it by her grandmother.

The side-road, which had been rising steadily and steeply, levelled out and ended in a transverse track scarcely fit to be called a road. Beyond this lay a stretch of open grass dotted with clumps of furze; and beyond that, far below, the sea sparkled in the sun.

A straggle of bungalows lined the inland side of the track, but the only building on the seaward side—and the only one of any size in sight—was a big red-and-white house with a glass-walled observation turret on its roof, perhaps a hundred yards away to the left. On the short drive leading to its front door stood the jeep. Kendrick drove onto the grass, stopped at a respectful distance from the unfenced cliff-edge, and settled to wait.

As on the previous evening, his receiver could get only Radio Samantha. He kept the volume down, for somebody's brass section was beating the daylights out of *Kiss Me Goodnight, But Don't Go*. And then the disc ended, and a very distinctive voice said, "Deeg zet crezzy trompet!" Startled, Kendrick turned up the volume. "Zees ees Zhuke-box Zhulie," said the voice, and he closed his eyes the better to concentrate as it went on to do a cosmetic plug and then announce another record. By that time he was quite certain. If he knew a voice from a velocipede, Juke-box Julie was the "kid sister" who had answered Hadley's phone. Could he be wrong about the pirate station's being a ship?

He opened his eyes again as the music started, and saw Inez standing beside the jeep. There was a tall man with her, and Kendrick raised his glasses. It was with satisfaction rather than surprise that he recognized John Doe.

FOURTEEN

By the end of an hour Kendrick concluded that, if La Zingara's letter had indeed been a "Panic Stations" call, the panic had not spread; not visibly, at all events, though of course there might have been phone-calls. Inez had long since disappeared in the jeep, John Doe had gone back into the house looking no more than thoughtful, and after that there had been nothing but sunshine, ozone, seagulls and, till a male colleague took over from her, Juke-box Julie.

Her voice was not only distinctive, he thought, but adorable, and he wondered if the rest of her matched it. It might be fun to find out sometime. Obviously one wouldn't ask Hadley for an introduction, but to a columnist such meetings are rarely hard to arrange. He already had her phone number, for a start . . .

An open Sunbeam convertible came up the road, its sole occupant a chic, middle-aged woman he had never seen before. Leaving the car where the jeep had been she went into the house, carrying a laden shopping-bag. She looked wholly un-panicstricken, and was almost certainly, he felt, Mrs. Doe getting home to see about lunch. And not a bad idea at that. He turned the Humber and drove back to his hotel to have some himself.

So he had located John Doe in spite of the Lewes registration clerk; and there seemed a fair chance that he had also located Carlos Urquiza's hideout. He had noticed, while Inez was telling him where her caravan had rested, that all the resorts she mentioned were in Sussex. It therefore seemed reasonable that the exiled rebel would be in Sussex too, near his post office; and where more safely than in that isolated villa with its roof-top watchtower and, no doubt, some kind of goat-track down the cliff behind it for emergency use?

He had located John Doe. And that very night, given any kind of luck, he would call on the man as the man had called on him—unannounced. But first it might be well to case the joint.

King Harold Helicopters Limited (proprietor Harold King, oddly enough) had its office in a wooden hut near the Hastings fish market, and its one and only chopper on a tarmac square alongside. Business was slack, and Kendrick's request for a solo charter was warmly welcomed. "Where would you like to go first, sir?" asked the pilot as they took off.

During lunch the journalist had enquired about Radio Samantha, and had been told that it was indeed a ship, as he had originally thought. It lay "somewhere out there," according to the waitress, who had accompanied the words with a sweeping gesture that included everything from Calais to Cherbourg. Now, as he pondered the pilot's question, he decided not only that it would be a mistake to go too directly to the real purpose of his flight, but also that it would be interesting to see where Julie spun her platters—perhaps even to get a glimpse of the girl herself, relaxing on deck before her next stint at the microphone. "Is the *Samantha* anywhere near here?" he asked.

The pilot said the *Samantha* was too unprintably near for comfort, and that it was practically impossible in this area to avoid interference from her pedicular programmes. But if Kendrick wanted to look at the adjectivally modified noun, fine. They flew out to sea, and the farther they flew the more Kendrick wondered how Julie contrived to commute between Piccadilly and mid-Channel. Maybe, of course, she spent alternate spells in each, and he had simply happened to catch her just before the changeover. "I suppose they operate the same way as Radio Caroline and the others?" he said. "Resident disc jockeys and thousands of records aboard?"

The pilot shook his head. "Everything's taped on shore," he said, "and sent out from Folkestone with the stores. There was a long piece about her in the *Sunday Bulletin* back in July, when she first started . . . There she is now."

Through the glasses Kendrick saw a small but extremely graceful vessel riding at anchor, her clipper bow pointing into the wind and her white hull shining. Except for the outsize radio mast she looked like, and probably had been, a yacht. Her house-flag was a green "R.S." monogram on white, but the national flag at her stern puzzled him. "Who owns her?" he asked. "That's not the Irish flag."

"It's Liechtenstein," said the pilot, grinning. "I suppose the company's registered there for tax reasons, but who they are I don't know."

They circled the little ship twice without seeing any sign of life, and then Kendrick said, "Okay. So much for *Samantha*. Let's have a look at some land now."

They came in over the Kent coast at Dunge Ness and the dreary flatness around Lydd, flew across Rye Bay, and then skimmed along the Sussex cliffs. John Doe's house came in view, and Kendrick saw that it did indeed have a seaward exit, and no mere goat-track either. Steps cut in the sloping cliff-face zigzagged down—with a wire-rope handrail beside them —to a concrete jetty in a small cove where a silver-grey motor-boat lay at moorings.

"It's the old Furzehill coastguard station," said the pilot in answer to his question. "Stood empty for a long time after they moved, but some Londoner bought it last year and converted it into a house."

"It's a marvellous situation," said the journalist. "Let's circle it and have a closer look."

He was studying the place intently as they approached it, assessing possible modes of entry, and was therefore quite unprepared for the pilot's soft wolf-whistle and murmur of, "Gosh, what a dish!"

Turning his head Kendrick too saw the dish, and the sight did something to the back of his throat. On a hedged-in patch of lawn, wearing the same sun-halter and tiny shorts she had worn that first morning on the *Duchess of Malfi*, sat Manuela. Inevitably, she was sewing, but she looked up at the chopper as it passed over her, and Kendrick quickly jerked back his head and forced himself to concentrate on the building. There was a flat-roofed outhouse there, with a window in the main wall above it, and . . .

"Hasn't been anything like that on the beach all summer," said the pilot. "Care to go round again, a bit lower?"

"I don't think so, thanks. I've never been much of a girl-watcher. It's too frustrating."

"You're probably right," said the pilot without conviction, and headed west again.

From Hastings Kendrick drove back to his hotel and changed into a dark grey suit and silent-soled hush-puppies, as being appropriate for the project he had in mind. The sight of Manuela sitting alone in the garden had somewhat shaken his theory that Urquiza might be at the old coastguard station—if he was, why the heck wasn't he by the side of his *querida?*— but had in no way lessened his urge to get into the place. One way or another he was determined to get a story over which Bill Hadley could have no conceivable power of veto.

There was no point in going near Furzehill before nightfall, of course, and this left him with time to kill. On an impulse he drove to the Pleasure Dome, but Madame Zingara's "Closed" sign was still in position. He headed inland for the caravan site.

It had occurred to him that Inez, though clearly not in Grandma's confidence, was certainly prying into the old lady's less public activities, and that this morning's letter might not be the first she had opened and read. If he could somehow shake her loose from the fortune-teller for an hour or so, it would be interesting to see what a mixture of charm and bribery might elicit. Nothing, quite possibly; but there was no harm in trying.

He had prepared a plausible approach by the time he reached the caravan, but was given no chance of using it. There was no reply to his knock.

"I'm afraid they're out," said a voice, and he turned to see an attractive young woman in a taut sweater standing in the doorway of the next trailer, the one he had watched Hadley enter. Another of the diplomat's kid sisters, maybe?

"You don't know where they went, do you?" he asked.

"I don't. They left about an hour ago, but—"

"Someone call for them, or did they just go off together on their own?"

The woman studied him for a moment, then said, "They didn't exactly go off together, they . . . well, one shouldn't gossip about the neighbours, I suppose, but if I don't tell you no doubt some of the other campers will. I'm sorry to say that the ladies had a flaming brawl in there this afternoon—smashing dishes and yelling at each other in Romany—it was awful. You could hear them all over the site. About a dozen of us were standing outside, discussing whether we should try to break it up before someone got hurt, when suddenly the girl came stamping out, barged through us and drove off in the jeep. Then Madame Zingara appeared, shouting, 'Stop her! Don't let her leave!', so my husband and another man offered to give chase, and asked the old witch if she'd like to go along. She went; and that's the last I've seen or heard of them."

"I see," said Kendrick thoughtfully. "Tell me, is your husband Bill Hadley, or is Bill just the other man?"

The woman laughed and said, "So you *are* Don Kendrick! I thought you must be, but I didn't like to ask. No, my husband's Tim Drayton, and my name's Vivienne. Tim and I have been here for a week. Bill only came down this morning."

"Whose car are they in? Bill's?"

"Yes, the Cresta . . . I've no more idea when they'll be back than you have, Don, but if you'd care to wait . . ." She gestured invitingly towards the interior of the trailer; and there was that in her smile which told Kendrick the wait would not be a boring one.

"Thanks," he said, grinning, "but I'll take a rain check. They might come back too soon."

There was little point in speculating on the cause of the quarrel, he thought as he drove into Hastings again. Possibly Inez had let slip something that revealed her snooping activities. Possibly it had been merely the eruption of two Gypsy temperaments cooped up together too long in too little space. Possibly, indeed, they made exhibitions of themselves like this at regular intervals, and that was why Madame Zingara felt impelled to change neighbours every few weeks. He was sorry to have lost the chance of pumping Inez, but he had a feeling that the old coastguard station would prove a better bet anyway.

By the time he emerged from the Saxon Snackery with an assortment of sea-food and sausages under his belt, dusk was falling and the street-lamps were lit; a circumstance to which he owed the fact that, as he strolled along the sidewalk, he again saw Manuela without her seeing him. Through one of the light-zones passed the open convertible he had seen at Furzehill, with the same woman driving it, and Manuela by her side.

For a moment he thought of following—they might be on their way to meet Urquiza, for instance—but he knew that by the time he had reached the Humber and got clear of the car-park they could be on any one of four or five roads out of town. He dropped the idea, and contented himself with the thought that, temporarily at least, the household at Furzehill had been reduced by two; a heartening fact for the would-be breaker-and-enterer.

As he drove along the promenade he saw the coloured lights on the outer end of the pier grow dim and then vanish. Sea-mist, he realized, was rolling in from the Channel, and it was rolling fast. Soon the whole pier was blotted out, and then the roadway ahead became vague and shadowy and he switched over to his fog-lamps. The mist might prove useful at Furzehill, but it was not going to make getting there any easier. He was glad he had not tried to find and follow the convertible. This was no night for tailing anything smaller than a travelling cir-cus.

It took an age to reach the T-junction where Inez had stopped that morning; but then, halfway up the side-road, he came suddenly into clear though dying light. He was above the mist.

He was also, he found, on the wrong side of the road, and he pulled over to avoid a Rover 2000 that was coming downhill. Who was in it he could not see, but his heart rejoiced as he read the number-plate. If John Doe too was going out for the evening, the old coastguard station might be almost or even quite empty. He thought of Vivienne Drayton back at her caravan, and told himself smugly that it looked as if his virtu-ous behaviour was going to pay off.

Lights showed in some of the bungalows on the dirt road, but he could see none—apart from an outside porch light—at the big house. He parked the Humber alongside a huge clump of gorse and switched off his lights, hoping to be taken—if any-one noticed the car at all—for a courting couple. Twenty min-utes later he judged it dark enough to slip out and make his way to his objective.

A circuit of the house disclosed another outside light, over a back door this time, but none within. Unless somebody was watching television in a darkened room, the place really did seem to be unoccupied. How long it might remain so, of course, there was no guessing. He had better not waste time.

The flat-roofed outhouse presented little difficulty, and the catch of the window above it yielded gracefully to his penknife. He climbed through, flicked on his flashlight, and found that he was on a carpeted landing, looking downstairs into a fair-sized entrance hall. For thirty seconds he stood there, straining his ears, but heard no sound of television. Reassured, he walked up to the next floor.

There were five bedrooms and three bathrooms on it, but two of the five had empty closets and chests of drawers. A third smelt evocatively of *Emeraude,* and he saw Manuela's shorts and sun-halter lying on a chair. But there was nothing to suggest that her Carlos had ever been there.

Next door was clearly what house-agents call "the master bedroom," and in its wardrobes he found clothes for both sexes, including the tweed suit John Doe had worn on Saturday. The fifth room had strictly feminine toiletries on its dressing-table; and that was that.

He ascended a narrower stair to the next floor and found a further three rooms, but two of them were unfurnished and the other had a maid's uniform hanging in the closet. Yet another ascent took him only to the glass-walled watchtower, from which he retreated fast. Unless they were hiding Carlos in the cellar, which seemed unlikely, or had given him accommodation in one of the public rooms on the ground floor, which did not seem very likely either, the man did not appear to be here. As Kendrick had practically reached that opinion already, he was not unduly disappointed. He went downstairs, looking for John Doe's desk.

It was in an oak-and-leather study with rich, thick drapes at the window. Kendrick, after a moment's hesitation, decided to draw them and risk the reading-lamp on the desk; and by its light he began his search.

Drawer 1 contained headed notepaper, both private and business, from which he learned that the converted coastguard station was now, rather uninspiredly, "Clifflands," and that Mr. Doe apparently had some connexion with London & Global

Oil Enterprises, Limited. Drawer 2 contained pencils, erasers, scissors, tape and gum. Drawer 3 contained manila folders, but before he could lift one out he heard the door creak behind him.

He swung round in the swivel-chair, and his heart missed a beat. Standing two yards away was the biggest Alsatian wolf-hound he had ever seen. As its eyes met his, it leapt.

FIFTEEN

Kendrick flung up his left arm defensively and felt sharp fangs stab into it. The wolfhound dropped back, and its weight pulled him to his knees on the floor, his arm firmly and painfully prisoned. There was a low, rumbling growl coming from deep inside the brute, but apart from that the two might have been a still from a Rin-Tin-Tin movie. Then, somewhere distant, a woman called, "Jasûr! Supper, boy."

Jasûr, his jaws clamped on something more important than supper, paid no attention; but the voice stirred Kendrick to action. Presumably the woman and the dog had come in while he was upstairs, and there might be others with them; John Doe, perhaps, if he had not been in the Rover. He reached into his hip pocket and drew Alberdi's *Cabrito*.

The Alsatian's growl became louder and its grip even tighter, and the journalist damned the fact that you could not say, "Hands up!" to a hound. Nor, if you happened to be Don Kendrick, could you shoot one. He slipped the barrel of the revolver under the thin steel chain that encircled the massive neck, and started to twist, tourniquet fashion.

"Jasûr! Where are you, boy?" The voice was louder, perhaps nearer. Kendrick twisted more quickly, wondering whether his fingers or that well-sheathed windpipe would tire first. "Jasûr! Your sup—"

The voice cut off abruptly, and Kendrick thought *Hell! She's seen the light shining through the doorway.* But at that moment the tourniquet did its work. Choking, the Alsatian released him; and, using both hands now, he gave the *Cabrito* another turn. If he could put the beast out for even a few seconds, he might still . . .

"Let him go or I'll put a bullet in you," the voice snapped from the doorway, and he heard the click of a gun being cocked.

Without raising his head from the threshing animal he said, "And get my throat torn out?"

The woman caught her breath and said, "Oh! It's you. All right, Jasûr, he's a friend . . . of sorts. He won't bite you now, Don. Let him go." For the first time, perhaps because until now he had been somewhat preoccupied, Kendrick recognized her voice.

"Okay, honey, if you say so," he said dubiously; released the Alsatian, and stood up to face the stormy eyes of Lynn Everett. She had a .22 rook-rifle trained on him.

"Come here, boy," she said. "If you've hurt him, Don . . ."

"The shoe's on the other paw," said Kendrick coldly, pocketing the pistol. He could feel blood trickling down his wrist onto his palm, and his wound pained him considerably. "Why we call these hellhounds 'shepherds' back home, I'll never know. That one could herd tigers. Incidentally, are you hiring out as an armed patrol these days, or what brings you here with your Baskervillean little pet?"

"Filial piety," said Lynn shortly, caressing the coughing beast. "This happens to be my home—as you could have found out long ago if you weren't so scared of meeting girls' parents; and more recently if my revered father didn't love to be mysterious. John Doe, for goodness' sake! I'm surprised it wasn't Fu Manchu or Dr. Moriarty."

Kendrick, as has been mentioned, was a good poker player, and his amazement scarcely showed. "Why wasn't it simply Mr. Everett?" he asked.

"Oh, Heaven knows! I think he had some crazy idea that it would embarrass you."

"To discover I was dating a burglar's daughter?"

"No, a girl whose father knew all about Mrs. Gomez."

The topic, Kendrick felt, was due for changing. "I like this carpet," he said, "but it's really too good for bleeding to death on. Do you have any old threadbare ones anywhere?"

"I'll look at your arm in a minute," said the girl. "As soon as Jasûr's fit to eat his supper." The Alsatian, who had stopped wheezing, wagged his tail; and Lynn, having seen him set to with enthusiasm on a high-piled dish, took Kendrick upstairs for treatment.

While she bathed, disinfected and dressed the forearm, she explained her presence at Clifflands. She had recognized her father, she said, from the description given to Tony Dane by the porter at Castlemaine Court; and, putting two and two together, had come up with a total of six, and the conviction that father was quite possibly involved in the kidnapping if not in the wrecking of the flat. She had accordingly wangled some leave and headed for home and a showdown.

"Thank you, honey," said the journalist gratefully.

"I didn't do it for *your* sake," said Lynn. "I only wanted to keep Daddy out of jail if I could." Learning that in fact Daddy was blameless, and then reading in the *Post* that Kendrick was safe and sound, she had been about to return to duty. But her mother had persuaded her to remain for another day or two and help her to entertain their Latin guest. Mother and guest had gone to a show in Eastbourne that evening, in case he was wondering, and with so much mist around they probably wouldn't be back this side of midnight, but of course if he cared to wait . . .

"When you tried to scare me off meddling with an English angle on Colombian politics," said Kendrick, firmly steering the conversation away from Manuela, "I suppose you only did it to keep me from butting in on your father's schemes?"

This, Lynn admitted, was so. Though officially retired, Hugh Everett was still on the board of his old company, and occasionally dabbed a finger into one or other of its pies, preferably a disreputable one. Lynn had guessed that he was up to something surreptitious and probably illegal in connexion with Colombian oil, but as a law-abiding civil servant she had asked no questions, feeling that the less she knew, the better.

Kendrick doubted that this was strictly true, but realized that the girl was going to tell him nothing of her father's business. And that her father himself would be more informative seemed improbable. As John Doe, he had made his views on publicity quite clear. The phrase "a bloody journalist" recurred to mind . . . Oh, if only he had been able to go through the man's desk!

With a neat bandage round his throbbing arm, Kendrick followed Lynn downstairs to a comfortably furnished lounge, gratefully accepted a large whisky, and sank into a welcoming chair. The girl, having checked Jasûr's plate and found it licked clean, admitted that possibly the dog had taken no lasting harm from his manhandling, and provisionally forgave Kendrick for defending himself. Even Jasûr, curled up beside her on the settee, seemed to have put the incident out of mind, for he yawned frighteningly twice and then fell asleep.

It was to this pleasantly domestic scene that Hugh Everett entered a few minutes later. If he was taken aback to see the visitor he recovered quickly, and managed a friendly smile.

"You've met Don, haven't you, Daddy?" said Lynn in her most social manner. "He was passing, so he thought he'd drop in. Through a window."

"I didn't have any skeleton keys," said Kendrick apologetically, shaking hands with his host.

"You're very welcome," said Hugh Everett. "Lynn, dear, this being Peggy's night off, do you think you could find me something to eat?"

"Of course," said the girl, and, having vainly offered Kendrick a snack, retired to the kitchen; which was perhaps the object of the exercise, for her father immediately said, "Don, where exactly do you stand in this business?"

"On the other side of the fence, I suspect. I'm a reporter, and I'm longing to report."

The late John Doe nodded. "Which would pay you better professionally," he asked, "to print what you already know, or at least as much of it as you can substantiate; or to sit on it, and perhaps on more besides, with the reasonable prospect of one day being *persona* very *grata* indeed to a South American president?"

Kendrick considered this, then said, "I have to decide right now?"

"N-no," said Everett, "I don't think you have. Either way, I'm sure you'll play fair with us . . . I don't suppose you'll tell me how the devil you found out about the Zingara set-up?"

"Information received. I got a tip that Carlos Urquiza was in England, and that the old girl was almost certainly acting as a post office for him, so I dropped in to talk to her. I didn't foresee that she'd recognize me, though, and write to you about it."

There was an odd expression in Everett's eyes that the younger man could not interpret, but his tone was perfectly normal when he said, "She was rather shaken by your obvious reference to Manuela. You see, Madame Zingara has no idea that Manuela is in this country, or even expected to arrive in it. Nor, for that matter, has Carlos, and it would be a considerable shock to him if he knew she was actually here. And frankly I wish to God she wasn't." Kendrick looked blank, and Everett said, "How much do you know about Manuela's background, Don—apart from what I told you on Saturday?"

"She's the Colonel's *querida,* and that letter you pinched from Sloane Square is the blueprint for a new *norteño* rising," said Kendrick promptly, and not without satisfaction. "At a guess, I'd say the boys have their sights set a little higher this time—on a breakaway republic, perhaps, with love in its heart for London & Global Oil."

Hugh Everett drew a deep breath, then smiled wryly. "Lynn

told me once," he said, "that socially you were a wolf, privately a lamb, and professionally a ferret. I can certainly endorse the last bit. Still, it makes it simpler to tell you the rest. Carlos Urquiza's a fairly typical Latin, Don, by which I mean that he'd sooner go without food than without women. He's had a string of them since he arrived here, and at present he's shacked up with yet another. It'll wear off in time, of course, but Manuela keeps asking me where he is and how soon she can meet him; and if he's not quite ready to change partners again . . ."

"She'll stick her little dagger in his black two-timing heart?"

"Lord, no, that's the last thing she'd do. But she might easily stick one in the girl. How deep her feelings for Carlos may be I don't know, but I do know that she hopes to marry him and become First Lady of the new republic. She's quite open about it. She told me that that was why she persuaded her fellow-conspirators to let her be the one to bring over the draft plans —so that she could rejoin Carlos in England and get a head start on any competition that might arise when he became President. By the time they told us who they were sending it was too late to stop her . . . Don, do you happen to know where Madame Zingara is?"

The abrupt change of subject took Kendrick by surprise. He frowned and said, "No. Isn't she back at the caravan yet?"

"She's not, although I sent word that I'd be round to see her. Where did she go to, do you know?"

Briefly, Kendrick gave him the gist of Vivienne Drayton's story. Hugh Everett was horrified. "Dear God!" he said. "You mean the Hadley who was on the *Duchess of Malfi?* Said he was coming back from a spell with the C.B.C.?"

"That's the guy."

"When Frank Farrell's office checked with the C.B.C. they denied all knowledge of him."

"Yes, it was only a front. He'd been sent out by the Foreign Office to—"

"No he hadn't. I wondered if he was a British agent, so I

made some discreet enquiries at a fairly high level. The F.O. knew nothing about him, suggested that he was merely a line-shooter, or at worst perhaps a confidence man. But I had a hunch that his play for Manuela might be more than it seemed, and that's why I pulled a few strings to have her disembarked unobtrusively, and then got her under cover."

Kendrick was puzzled. "If he's not an F.O. man," he began, and then another thought struck him, and he felt slightly sick. "When did Farrell find out that Hadley was unknown at C.B.C.?" he asked.

"He got a cable from his office on the Tuesday evening, and phoned me from the ship. He wanted to discuss it with some-one, and Manuela was too ill to see him."

"And before she could recover he'd gone over the side," said Kendrick bleakly. "And Bill Hadley had a contact in the Purs-er's Bureau who no doubt passed on the contents of any in-teresting telegrams. Hell, what a sucker I've been!" Briefly he explained just how, and wound up with, "There was I, swallow-ing everything he told me; and all the time it was almost cer-tainly he who blackjacked me before helping Clancy to toss Farrell in the drink!"

The older man nodded. "A temporary alliance for a com-mon end, probably," he said. "From what you tell me, it suited both Hadley and Clancy to have Farrell out of the way, and their principal aims didn't clash. Apparently all Clancy wanted were the papers Manuela was carrying, and Hadley didn't care about those so long as he got his lead to Carlos Urquiza."

"But if he's not F.O. why should he want to find Urquiza? Unless of course he's working for the Colombian Government. Think he is?"

"I doubt it," said Everett. "A Colombian agent who located Carlos would only have to report him to the British police to have him repatriated through the normal legal channels. I don't think he'd undermine his own position by doing anything as lawless as kidnapping—which Hadley appears to have done to-night."

"Madame Zingara, you mean? Yes, it looks rather like it. Do you think she'll break down and tell him where Carlos is?"

Everett gave an odd, unhappy little smile. "That quarrel in the caravan," he said, "couldn't have been in Romany. It must have been in Spanish, which Manuela says Hadley speaks fluently. As he evidently overheard the whole thing, he probably realized where Carlos was, because in private Inez would use the masculine forms of address. Madame Zingara *is* Carlos, Don, and Inez is the current girl friend. As a matter of fact, when I heard you'd gone to the Dome, I thought you must have found out somehow."

The entrance of Lynn with a tray gave Kendrick a chance to adjust himself to the bombshell. He accepted a refill of his whisky glass, noted that the alcohol was already abating the pain in his arm, and said, "I presume that letter you got this morning made the Manuela/Carlos relationship pretty obvious?"

"Yes," said Everett. "Why?"

"Inez read it on her way here, so now we can guess what started the fight." He was silent for a few seconds. "Okay," he said. "So Hadley wanted to kidnap Carlos, and apparently he's succeeded. But why? If he's neither a British nor a Colombian agent, what the deuce is he?"

"If he's kidnapped Carlos," said Lynn, "he's probably one of the Mercenaries."

"The who?"

"That's just a name the F.O. has given them for convenient reference. They are, as far as we can discover, an organized but completely freelance group of . . . agents is a very vague word, but I can't think of another one. They own no national allegiance, simply sell their information and services in the best market. They'll spy on their own countries just as readily as—"

"Do they kidnap people?"

"They've tracked down a few war criminals and sold them to

Bonn and Israel, so they might well hope to sell Urquiza to Bogotà. But how and when was he kidnapped?"

While her father brought her up to date, Kendrick considered this new aspect of the situation. And, as he did so, it occurred to him that one or two seemingly unimportant facts might have more significance than he had thought, and that an apparent inconsistency in financial policy might well be more intelligent than it looked. The odds were a hundred to one against his guess being right, he told himself, but still . . .

"Mind if I use your phone?" he asked.

Lynn led him to a telephone in a cloakroom off the hall and left him there. He phoned the *Bulletin* office and then, having been given a name and a Folkestone number, phoned that. For a time he asked questions and received answers which seemed to please him, and then he read off the Everett number from the instrument and said, "You'll call me back even if it's a nil report? . . . Thanks a lot." He hung up and returned to the lounge.

"There's probably nothing to this at all," he said, "but it struck me that Hadley wouldn't have chosen the role of a radio man if he hadn't the technical knowledge to back it up in conversation, so that the chances were he did have some background of radio experience. Then it struck me that his *querida* or *inamorata* or *petite amie* or whatever—I don't know her nationality—is a lady disc jockey called Juke-box Julie."

"You do get around, don't you?" said Lynn.

"I've never even seen the girl," said Kendrick loftily.

"Isn't she on that pestilential pirate?" asked Everett. "Radio Samantha?"

"Theoretically," said Kendrick, "yes, she is. Factually, no, she's not. All the programmes are taped in London. Now, it's far cheaper to broadcast discs direct from a turntable than it is to re-record them first, so it seems on the face of it a rather spendthrift way of doing business—and inconsistently so, for a concern that has taken the trouble to register its headquarters in one of the low-taxation countries. But of course it's ideal if you want to keep the ship's company to a minimum. Officially, I've just been told, the only people on the *Samantha* are three engineers."

"Why do you say 'officially'?" asked Lynn.

"Because, honeybun, another thought had occurred to me. As you probably know, Radio Samantha is, physically, a converted yacht lying off Kent, well outside the three-mile territorial limit. Legally, however, it's a little bit of Liechtenstein; and if the British police, for instance, tried to go on board uninvited, that would technically be invasion of a sovereign state. I simply thought it would be a useful hideout for an international gang, be they your Mercenaries or not. I don't know how you'd set about extraditing somebody from Liechtenstein, in fact I'm not quite sure where Liechtenstein is, but—"

"In the Alps between Switzerland and Austria," said Lynn, showing signs of interest. "Sixtytwo square miles of it, and, as you say, a low-taxation country; for which reason it's chockfull of international holding companies. Donnie-boy, I believe you could be onto something—about the *Samantha,* I mean, as a sanctuary for spies."

"Apart from anything else," said Everett, also showing signs of interest, "a radio station would be the perfect cover for a secret transmitter—Poe's 'Purloined Letter' principle. And the yacht, as a staging point, would greatly simplify the business of smuggling people in and out of Britain. By jove, Don! Do you think . . ."

"I'm not allowing myself to," said Kendrick. "It's all far too conditional at the moment. But *if* the yacht is more sinister than it seems to be, and *if* Hadley is connected with it, then I can't imagine a better place to cache Urquiza till they can arrange onward transmission. Which may take some time, for today's snatch can't have been a planned affair—only sheer opportunism. But it's if, if, if all down the line; and let's face it —the odds are that the darn boat's nothing more than just a radio pirate."

"So what do you suggest we do?" asked Everett.

"I'm waiting for a phone-call. The *Bulletin* carried a fairly detailed article on *Samantha* while I was in South America, I gather, and I've just been talking to the chap who wrote it—our man in Folkestone. Apparently the tender that services the yacht belongs to his father-in-law—that's how he came to get shown over her when she first went into business—so he's going to see if he can find out anything, and call me back."

"In that case," said Everett, looking happier than he had done for some time, "I'll ask you to excuse me. I'm going out for a few minutes, Lynn." Hopefully, Jasûr jumped down and followed him. Also hopefully, Kendrick strolled over and took the dog's vacated place beside Lynn.

"Care for a game of cribbage while we're waiting, Don?" asked the girl.

"I must admit," said Kendrick, letting his arm rest on the back of the settee, "that the idea hadn't occurred to me."

"All right," said Lynn agreeably, "we'll just talk. Oh, wasn't that an awfully good picture of you in today's *Courier?* You know, peering down the front of your friend's frock? I had thought Yousuf Karsh was about the only photographer who could capture a sitter's soul, but—"

"Okay, lass, I read you," said Kendrick, grinning and getting to his feet again. "We play cribbage."

They had barely completed their first game, however, when the call from Folkestone came through. It lasted some minutes, during most of which Kendrick merely listened. Then he went back to the lounge, to find that Hugh Everett had returned.

"It appears," he said, "that in addition to renting father-in-law's tender to deliver fuel and other heavy stores, the *Samantha* people keep a motor launch at the same boatyard. It's one of the yacht's lifeboats. Tonight at six . . . how far is Folkestone from that caravan park, Mr. Everett?"

"Oh . . . Fifty miles, perhaps."

"Then it fits very nicely for time. Tonight at six the company's Sales Manager arrived at the yard and collected the launch to take a couple of shareholders out for a look at *Samantha*. He said he'd be picking them up farther along the waterfront, and that if the fog came down as it did last night they'd all sleep on the yacht, so father-in-law wasn't to worry about them. Like it?"

"Very much," said Everett.

"So do I. I'd say there's a reasonable chance that the Sales Manager is either Bill Hadley or his friend Tim Drayton, and that the third man's Urquiza. If I'm right . . . I imagine, Mr. Everett, that London & Global's cloak and dagger department can produce a few muscle boys if and when the need arises?"

"It can," said Everett with a slight smile. "And will."

"For Heaven's sake!" said Lynn. "You can't go invading a foreign country on the off-chance that Urquiza's in it. And that's what you're suggesting—that or piracy."

"Not on the off-chance, I agree," said Kendrick. "We'd have to be sure first that he was there, naturally. So I thought if we could get a motorboat, and a portable radio that we could align on *Samantha*'s transmitter, we could probably locate her in spite of the fog, and I could go aboard and have a look-see."

Lynn's expression indicated no great enthusiasm for the scheme, but her father nodded approval. "My boat's in the cove," he said. "I've just been down checking her over in case we'd want her. And we don't need a portable radio—she has a built-in direction-finding one."

"Assuming that we do locate the yacht," said Lynn, "and that you manage to board her, Don—what happens if you're caught?"

"If she's only what she claims to be after all, then I'm an over-enthusiastic pressman looking for a story. I apologize for my intrusion, and withdraw."

"But if she's what you suspect she is?"

Kendrick was silent for a few moments. Then he smiled faintly. "In that event," he said, "I don't apologize."

SIXTEEN

On the cliff-top the night was clear, but below, where the stars should have been reflected, stretched a sky-to-sky carpet of charcoal grey. Halfway down the steps they were in it, and by the time they reached sea-level visibility was measurable in feet rather than yards.

"Her name's *Zibaq*," said Hugh Everett, indicating the motorboat Kendrick had seen at moorings that afternoon. It was now alongside the jetty; a trim, twentytwo foot inboard job with a roofed wheelhouse forward.

"Want to get under cover, Don?" asked Lynn, stepping on board and turning aft. "Or will you stay out here with me on the fog deck?" She sat down in the stern sheets.

"The silly questions you ask!" said Kendrick, jumping into the rocking boat and joining her. Everett cast off, and went into the wheelhouse.

"The beauty of the direction-finder," he said, "is that you don't have to listen to the signal the whole time. You get roughly on the beam by ear, fine-tune it with the decibel-meter, and then simply hold your compass course with an occasional sound-correction for drift." He switched on the engine and donned a pair of earphones. As the boat nosed out of the cove he swung her bow in a gentle arc, checked, swung back a few degrees, then held her steady while he studied the meter. "There or thereabouts, I think," he said, removing the earphones. "Practically due east, so when we want to get home again we just go west."

"We'll be lucky if we don't go west before that," said Lynn.

"Sounds like a lot of traffic in the Channel tonight, and it wouldn't take much to slice through this little eggshell."

"What I love about you is your unfailing cheerfulness," said Kendrick. But he too had been listening to the medley of distant foghorns, and wondering just how busy the shipping lanes might be.

"Most of these fellows are probably at anchor," said Everett hopefully from the wheelhouse. "I doubt if there'll be much movement tonight, except maybe a few big ones whose navigation bridges are high enough to be in the clear."

"A few big ones is all we need," said Lynn, and the conversation languished.

Calculating from the Folkestone man's estimate of *Samantha*'s position, Everett had reckoned her to be—at the maximum safe speed in this weather—some two and a half hours away; which should bring them to her with time in hand before her transmitter closed down at one a.m. But now Kendrick found himself wondering what would happen if the calculation proved to be a mile or two out, or if tides and currents slowed *Zibaq* below the speed her owner thought he was making.

Unless they found the yacht by one o'clock they would never find her at all, he was quite certain. In this visibility it would be sheer luck if you found the *Queen Elizabeth*. And although the Straits of Dover might look tiny on the map, they offered plenty of scope for losing yourself in a fog. He wondered how much gas they had in the tank, and then resolved that he must not let the weather seep into his soul. He drew Lynn close to him, nibbled her ear, and murmured, "What a darned shame it's too dark to play cribbage!"

Time passed, and the increased swell told them, if nothing else did, that they had left the shore well behind. There was no wind, strictly speaking, but occasional air currents made the mist eddy and drift and sometimes clear briefly altogether. On one such occasion they sighted a small coaster with riding-lights fore and aft, but apart from her they had so far seen nothing—nothing but vague shapes that faded or disintegrated as the mist swirled. It was all rather eerie, and the chilly damp did not help.

Foghorns continued to sound near and far, and once they heard seven bells being made aboard some invisible vessel. "Eleven-thirty," said Kendrick, and wondered if they were still on schedule. Everett had been varying his speed to match the visibility, and it was quite impossible to guess what he was averaging.

They were in a moderately thick patch when Kendrick thought he heard a new noise above the throb of the motor. He listened for a few seconds and then said, "There's a ship coming up, somewhere to port."

"I hear her," said Everett. "And she's coming fast, damn her." The sound of turbines was quite plain now, and all three strained their eyes, seeking its source. A foghorn boomed, they heard the swish of a bow-wave, and then suddenly through the mist came a high, raked stem that appeared to be racing straight at them.

Everett spun his wheel hard over and the engine-note surged to a roar, but for seconds that felt like hours *Zibaq* seemed not to be answering. Then, as the great black bows loomed above her, she swung round with a stomach-turning heel and shot away. Moments later she was tossing wildly in the liner's wash, and Kendrick was picking Lynn up from the floorboards. "That guy," he said shortly, "ought to be shot."

Lynn gave a venomous look at the towering shape that was already disappearing into the mist. "If I ever find out who he is," she said, "he will be. If he was doing one knot he was doing forty."

Her father smiled. "About sixteen, I'd estimate," he said. "But it's still far too fast for these conditions. And he's miles too close to shore. Probably the fog's worse farther out." He donned the earphones again for a minute and returned *Zibaq* to her course.

More time passed. The mist became pearly overhead, and they knew that the moon must be up. "Any idea how far we've come, Skipper?" Kendrick asked.

"Roughly eighteen miles," said Everett. He put on the earphones, then added, "And from the strength of the signal we must be pretty well there." He listened for a time, then took them off. "Juke-box Julie doing her stuff," he announced. "That's a fascinating accent she has, Don."

"Sure is," Kendrick agreed. "But right now I'm more interested in her fascinating boy friend. Skip, I've been hearing a foghorn grow louder for the past few minutes, and it sounds like straight ahead. Think it could be *Samantha* at last?"

"Quite possibly," said Everett. "Anyway, we'll go dead slow. I don't suppose they'll be keeping a deck watch, but there's no sense in taking chances."

The engine-note became barely audible as they glided through the mist. Each blast of the horn ahead was appreciably stronger than the one before, and after a time it was almost deafening. Then a vague patch of whiteness on the starboard bow resolved itself into the ghostly outline of the yacht. She was practically stern-on to them, perhaps thirty yards away.

There was no need for speech, because their procedure had been agreed hours before. The journalist wanted to make a complete circuit of the ship, close up, before attempting to board her. There might be a friendly rope hanging down somewhere, or even a Jacob's ladder if the launch from Folkestone was alongside. Failing all else he would climb up her anchor-chain and hope that the hawse-hole was not too far below deck level. But there might be an easier way.

Everett steered *Zibaq* to the stern of the yacht and switched off his engine, though the low pulsing of the ship's generators was probably loud enough to cover it. He locked the wheel, produced a single-bladed paddle and, while Lynn held a cork fender overside in case of a bump, propelled the boat forward. Kendrick, leaning outboard, pressed his hands against the ship's side and did his best to aid their slow progress. At intervals the foghorn above blared vibrantly.

Halfway along, Kendrick looked up and saw that a lifeboat was swung out on the davits; the launch from Folkestone, no doubt. So there would be no Jacob's ladder.

There was no friendly rope either, at least not on this side. They reached the graceful clipper bow and went past it until the journalist, standing upright, was able to grasp the anchor-chain. He held on, peering up it and trying to make out the hawse-hole; but the mist was much denser here, and the chain simply disappeared into it. How high the bow might stand he could not guess, but it was certainly much loftier than the stern.

And then suddenly a door slammed somewhere on deck, and a deep voice shouted, "Bill! You out here, by any chance?"

"Up for'ard, old boy." That was Hadley, and he was star-tlingly close. He must be right in the nose of the ship. The three scarcely breathed, although as they could not see him it was unlikely that he could see *Zibaq*.

Footsteps approached along the deck and the deep voice said, "Thick as ever. Light south-easterlies are forecast, Mac says, but whether they'll be strong enough to blow it away . . ."

"What's the latest from *Brynhild?*" asked Hadley.

"Still proceeding by guess and by God. Bernstorff's guess is that not even God could get her here before daylight, and of course if she hits anything—"

The foghorn blared, and when it ceased the deep voice said, "Holy hell! That thing's bad enough when you're inside, but out here it's pure murder."

"You get used to it," said Hadley. "No more news from Viv, I suppose?"

"No."

"I wish I knew what that damned Canuck was up to."

"What makes you think he's up to anything at all?"

"When a man acts out of character, Tim, I'm always sus-picious. Our little Vivienne is a very attractive wench, and Kendrick's no Joseph, but when she gave him the eye he took off like a startled fawn. Why?"

"Maybe he's really a clean-living all-Canadian boy at heart."

"Tim," said Hadley, "if that bloke found himself alone in the Louvre for five minutes he'd make a pass at the Mona Lisa." Kendrick sensed rather than heard Lynn's chuckle, and wished Hadley would shut up. "No, old boy, take it from me, when he ran away from Viv it was for some good reason. Either he guessed that she was trying to stop him from looking for us, or—"

"He couldn't possibly have known where to look."

"Well, then, he had some important project in hand, and I wish I knew what it was."

"Probably a previous date. I think you're worrying unnecessarily, Bill. He may still be trying to dig up a story, and in fact he may be hoping you'll relent and give him one, but if he even suspected that your F.O. act was phoney I'm sure an old hand like Viv would have spotted it in his manner. She's pretty sensitive to nuances, and—"

The foghorn intervened; and after it Tim Drayton said, "You can stay here if you like, but I'm getting indoors before that thing blasts off one more time. If I can find some cotton-wool for my ears I might even try to sleep. What about you?"

"N-no, not sleep, I think," said Hadley. "I want to be on hand in case the *Brynhild* arrangement has to be altered." A glowing cigarette-end shot out of the mist and hissed briefly in the water three feet from the motorboat. "But I'll go down and see how our guest's doing. He may have come to by now." Two sets of footsteps receded and a door slammed.

By signs Kendrick indicated his desire to check now on the starboard side of the yacht, and Everett paddled accordingly. The going was easier this time, for the tide was with them, but the result was the same; no ladder and no rope. When they were once again at the stern, Everett gave two strong strokes of the paddle, then shipped it and let the boat drift. Kendrick watched the yacht as it grew slowly fainter, and when it had faded from sight he said, "That's where I'm going in—by the back door. The little tail-piece right at the stern is much lower than I thought when I saw her from the air. If I stand on top of your wheelhouse, Skip, and time the rise and fall correctly, I should be able to get a grip and pull myself up."

This triggered an argument that was none the less violent for having to be conducted in a close huddle, and *sotto voce*.

Lynn's views were clear and forthright. Their trip had been purely a reconnaissance, she said, to establish whether or not Urquiza was a prisoner in the yacht. By a stroke of sheer luck they had eavesdropped on proof that he was, so now their obvious course was to return to base and take counsel with her father's nefarious associates. Kendrick's projected "look-see" was no longer necessary, and, in the circumstances, would be pushing their luck too far.

To this Kendrick replied that a council of war would be just dandy if they had time for it, but that it seemed possible the prisoner would be trans-shipped to some vessel called *Brynhild* soon after daylight, and might be halfway to Colombia before London & Global Oil could come up with a rescue team. The only course, as he saw it, was to try to spring the guy now; or, rather, about 1.30, by which time the engineering staff would probably be asleep—they were due to resume transmission at 6 a.m.—and Drayton too might have dropped off. "Leaving only Hadley," he ended reasonably.

"Armed, restless, and maybe not 'only' either," breathed Lynn fiercely. "He may have a dozen thugs on board, for all we know."

"I happen to be armed myself, and also they're not expecting me. Honey, I just have to go aboard. What do you think, Skip?"

Everett, who also "happened" to be armed, thought that both he and Kendrick should go aboard, thus halving the odds against them.

"And doubling the risk of discovery," said the journalist. "Besides, it would leave Lynn on her own." He caught sight of Lynn's expression, and dropped that line of argument.

Everett peered at his watch, then returned to the wheel-house and donned his earphones once more. He switched on the engine, keeping it to a barely audible minimum, and ma-noeuvred the boat slowly for a time, watching his instruments. Then he cut out the engine and stood silently for five minutes, listening and studying the compass. "And a gret beeg good-night keess to yourself, Zhulie," he murmured at last, and came aft. "Station closing down," he said, "but I've got a bearing on it and a fair idea of how we're drifting, so even if they stop the foghorn I ought to find her all right when we want to. How's the debate going?"

"It's over," said Lynn with a sigh, "through sheer weariness on my part. He just won't be talked out of going. Tell him your cock-eyed safety precaution, Don. He'll probably think it's just fine."

Shortly before two o'clock *Zibaq* again glided quietly up to *Samantha*'s stern. The yacht's generators had stopped, and apart from the regular braying of the foghorn the only sound was the occasional slap of water against her hull.

Kendrick, standing precariously astride the miniature searchlight on top of the wheelhouse, tensed himself as the gap narrowed between him and his target; then, as a wave lifted *Zibaq,* but before it could lift the yacht, he jumped. His hands closed on the teak handrail above him, and he hung limp against the counter, waiting for the next blast of the foghorn. When it came, drowning any sounds he might make, he pulled himself up and rolled aboard.

The "little tail-piece"—more properly the after-deck, he sup-posed—contained only a tarpaulin-covered winch and a cou-ple of bollards. A steep steel ladder led to the deck above, and in the bulkhead behind it there was a door, which proved im-movable. It was bolted on the inside, presumably, for there was no sign of a lock. Very cautiously, Kendrick climbed the ladder.

His Folkestone colleague had given him a detailed description of the vessel, and he knew that the superstructure ahead of him contained the former cocktail lounge, now the engineers' common room, and, forward of that but separated from it by the main companionway leading below, four deck-cabins. These had been the most luxurious staterooms on board in *Samantha*'s palmier days, so naturally the three radio engineers now occupied one each. The fourth had been turned into a radio shack, quite independent of the main transmitter, and used for short-wave communication between ship and shore.

The shack was to port, and Kendrick felt that it might well have somebody in it keeping touch with *Brynhild*, so he set off silently up the other side, *Cabrito* in hand. Apart from her riding lights the yacht seemed to be in darkness, but the mist had thinned somewhat and moonlight was filtering through. As he reached the foredeck he paused, holding his breath, for up in the bows a shadowy figure was leaning on the rail, looking out into the night. Apparently the restless Hadley had returned to his post.

Kendrick reversed his grip on the pistol, holding it club-fashion, and reflecting that it was exactly a week since Hadley had blackjacked him when he tried to follow Clancy and Farrell. *Happy anniversary, Bill* . . . The foghorn sounded, and under its cover he advanced to within two yards of the unsuspecting Englishman. But even as he went, the memory of Farrell suggested another idea. He transferred the gun to his left hand as the horn stopped. "So ya thought ya killed me?" he rasped, in a very passable imitation of the dead detective.

Hadley whirled round incredulously, and with infinite satisfaction Kendrick sank a right hook in his solar plexus. It jarred him to the elbow as it landed, but what it did to Hadley made up for much. The Englishman folded, and Kendrick lowered him quietly to the deck, where he gagged him with handkerchiefs and bound his wrists behind his back with his own expensive tie. At which point a Glasgow voice called from somewhere astern, "Mr. Hadley! . . . I've got old Bernstorff on again, if ye want him." That would be Mac, probably. "Mr. Hadley! . . . He must of went below, Bert." A door closed quietly.

Kendrick decided against tying Hadley's ankles. With at least two men up and alert, speed was of the essence, so he went swiftly through the unconscious man's pockets. Everett had given him a bunch of skeleton keys for use if and when he located Urquiza's prison, but if he could find the official one . . . This had to be it; an hotel-type key with a metal tag bearing the figure 5. He pocketed it and the pearl-handled Colt from Hadley's shoulder-holster, and set off aft. As he did so he felt a distinct breeze on his cheek. Mac's "light south-easterlies" appeared to be coming up.

He found the door to the main companionway and, remembering how it had slammed when Drayton and Hadley used it, closed it carefully behind him. The lighting within was dim but adequate. He tiptoed down, a step at a time, but heard nothing until the foghorn sounded again. Drayton had been quite right—the noise was not nearly so bad below decks.

Down here, he knew, were the dining-saloon and, abaft it, a double row of cabins lining a passage that ran right to the stern. No. 5 proved to be the first on the starboard side. He unlocked the door and peeped in.

Seated on the rumpled bunk, drawing on a cigarette, was a dejected-looking man in vest and underpants, who glanced up at him without interest or recognition. A swift look round the room showed that there was nobody else in it, so Kendrick stepped inside. A frock and a cardigan lay in one corner with a grey wig on top of them, and on the bedside table stood a rum bottle and a glass, both half full. The man's face was recognizably that of Madame Zingara, but there was no longer anything remotely feminine about it, nor did it look a day over forty.

"Cheer up, Colonel," said Kendrick in a low voice. "I'm the Army of Liberation."

Now recognition dawned, and the prisoner jerked back as if to avoid a blow. "You're Donald Kendrick," he said accusingly. There was no trace of the palmist's assumed huskiness. "Get out of here!"

"Keep your voice down, you imbecile! D'you want to have the whole mob round us? And what do you mean, get out of here?"

"I don't trust you, Kendrick. You're plotting against me."

"Will you lower your voice, for Pete's sake? This isn't a parade ground! I'm here to help you, you goon. Don't you want to be rescued?"

"Not by you."

Kendrick stared at him unbelievingly. This was impossible; it just couldn't be happening. And yet it was. "You'd rather be shipped back to Colombia?" he asked. "Stuck against a wall with a last cigarette, and a bandage over your eyes?"

"I'll get a fair trial, which is more than I'd get from you."

Kendrick looked at the bottle, and wondered. But no, nobody could be as drunk as this. And anyway, the man didn't sound drunk; only crazy. "Do you mean to say," he said, "that the Everetts and I—"

"What do you know about Everett?"

"Only that he's standing off in a motorboat waiting for me to bring you along. What do I tell him? That you decided to commit suicide instead?"

Urquiza studied him intently for a few moments, then shook his head with a contemptuous smile. "I don't believe you," he said. "You came to Bexhill today to spy on me, and I—"

"Well I'm damned!" said a deep voice. Kendrick swung round, and saw a stocky, broad-shouldered young man standing in the doorway. There was a look of unwilling admiration on his face and an unwavering automatic in his hand.

"Mr. Drayton, I presume?" said Kendrick; and then, glancing past the newcomer, "Why don't you introduce us properly, Viv?"

"Probably because she's not there," said Drayton without turning his head. "An oldie, Kendrick, and unworthy of you. But how the devil did you get here?"

"Swam."

"That you didn't, which means there's a boat out there to be taken care of, and pretty damn pronto too. But first things first. You have an unshapely bulge in your right-hand jacket pocket, my friend. Lift it out slowly with two fingers and toss it over here at my feet." Kendrick did as he was bidden, and Drayton's eyes narrowed. "That looks suspiciously like Bill's gun," he said. "So what's happened to Bill?"

"My friends are taking care of him till I get back to the boat."

Drayton eyed him thoughtfully. "I doubt it," he said at last. "But the fact that you got his gun away from him suggests that you must have one of your own. Turn round." Kendrick did not move. "Turn round, I said—unless you want a slug in your guts."

"It's only fair to tell you," said the Canadian, still without moving, "that if I don't reappear, safe and sound, by 2.30 a.m., my friends will send up enough distress rockets to bring every lifeboat and coastguard cutter in the area charging full speed at *Samantha*. And the fog's lifting, so full speed will be quite fast."

"That," said Drayton, "smells unpleasantly like the truth. All right, you're safe for the moment. But Urquiza isn't, for nobody can prove he was ever on board, and if he does have to go over the side with a chain necklace . . . Turn round, Kendrick, or the Colonel gets shot a little."

Kendrick turned round, and felt the *Cabrito* being taken from his hip pocket. Then the door banged and he heard the key turn. He looked witheringly at the Colonel. "Satisfied?" he asked.

"Kendrick, are you—are you really with Hugh Everett?"

"Yes, of course I am. And you'd be with him too by this time if you hadn't yelled your pointed head off and brought Drayton. I've a darned good mind to leave you here after all."

"No. No, Kendrick, please, if there's any way—"

"Then stop all that nonsense about my spying and plotting and do what you're told." He was looking through Everett's skeleton keys, seeking one of suitable size. The first two he tried were unsuccessful, but with the third the lock clicked back. Cautiously he looked out into the alleyway. It was empty. He jerked his head for Urquiza to follow him, closed the door quietly behind them and led the way aft.

The passage ended at a white-painted iron door which was bolted top and bottom—the door that gave on the little afterdeck. The upper bolt seemed immovable at first, but then it suddenly shot back with a report like a gun. Kendrick swore, and strained at the lower one, which was even stiffer and, when at length it yielded, louder.

As the steel mass creaked back on its hinges a genuine gun roared and reverberated at the other end of the passage, and they heard the bullet ricocheting all over the place. Kendrick bundled Urquiza out and pulled the door to, just as a second shot clanged on it. And then a voice said, "Stay right where y'are, boys, or I'll make bluidy pepper-pots o' ye. They're doon aft, Mr. Drayton." Looking up at the deck above, Kendrick saw a slim figure leaning over the rail, pointing a shotgun at him.

Running footsteps approached, and Drayton appeared at the rail. "Nice work, Mac," he said. "Get back inside, you two, or—"

A searchlight cut blindingly through the moonlit wisps of mist, illuminating the whole scene. "*Samantha* ahoy!" called an authoritative, megaphoned voice. "What the devil's going on?

We heard small-arms fire." For a frozen second nobody moved; and then, somewhere behind the searchlight, a .22 rifle cracked. Mac gave a yelp of pain, and his shotgun clattered down onto the after-deck.

As Kendrick dived for it he heard a pistol fire twice, and the searchlight went out. Then there was a loud splash, and he realized that he was alone on the after-deck. Even if *Zibaq*'s pseudo-official approach had fooled the enemy for a moment, Urquiza had obviously recognized Hugh Everett's voice, and taken prompt and appropriate action.

Standing back against the bulkhead Kendrick fired vertically, then ran out and turned, ready to fire again. But there was no need for the second barrel. Drayton and Mac were no longer visible, and he could hear their voices—plus Hadley's, he thought—from somewhere amidships. He tossed the shotgun overside, and followed it in a graceful arc.

Ten yards away he surfaced, in time to see Urquiza being hauled aboard *Zibaq*, so he struck out for her as strongly as his lounge-suit and shoes would allow. There were creaking and banging noises behind him, and then a minor thunderclap. He guessed that the swung-out lifeboat had been lowered—far too quickly, by the sound of it—and seconds later he heard its engine start up. By that time, though, he had got hold of *Zibaq*'s gunnel and was hoisting himself aboard. As he rolled into the well of the boat beside the panting Colombian, Everett gave the motor its head and Lynn's rook-rifle cracked twice. "I think I've winged another of them, Don," she said happily. "Oh, boy! I'm having a wonderful time."

"Then suppose you have it down here in cover, you blood-thirsty pygmy," said Kendrick, as something thudded into the motorboat's hull and they heard the report of the gun that had sent it there. "That's a *real* rifle they're using, Miss Oakley."

"I'm afraid you're right," said the girl regretfully. A bullet whistled past, followed by another report. "Yes, probably a .303 or something like that." She crouched down beside him, her eyes shining in the moonlight, and kissed his nose. "I'm so glad I didn't manage to talk you out of it," she said. They heard two more reports and another thud.

And then, abruptly, there was no moonlight, only the damp, swirling mist again. "Evasive action—I hope," said Hugh Everett. "I'd rather give them the slip than try to race them when we're out-ranged like that." He was giving the boat plenty of helm, Kendrick realized; and then they were on an even keel again, and another course. "The breeze is clearing the fog away, but this seems to be a pretty dense pocket. If it holds for a mile or two . . ." He stopped as the engine sputtered, coughed and died.

"What has happened?" asked Urquiza grimly.

Kendrick stood up and looked astern. Snaky traces of oil told their own story. "One of these shots hit the gas tank, I guess," he said quietly. "Stand by to repel boarders."

As they rocked helplessly in the swell they heard the engine of the *Samantha*'s launch grow steadily louder; then just as steadily fade. "Missed us," said Lynn, lowering her rifle.

"They'll be back," said Kendrick.

But the engine-note dwindled to silence, and the minutes passed without further sound of it. After a quarter of an hour Everett said, "I can't imagine where they've gone, but it seems to me, Lynn, that this would be a good time to break out the soup and the sandwiches. After which, if we're still unaccompanied, I'll switch to the emergency tank and carry on. It contains exactly one gallon, Carlos, so we'll have to crawl. But it ought to get us home sometime—barring accidents."

The rest of the journey was anti-climax. Urquiza, who had exchanged his wet underwear for a suit of denims and a pair of sneakers that Everett produced from the locker, sat shivering in the stern-sheets and spoke little. Kendrick, for his part, had elected to let his clothes dry on him, and a slow, cold process it was. The air temperature was several degrees lower than that of the sea.

The breeze freshened and the mist patches became increasingly few and wispy. Clouds hid the moon from time to time but visibility in general was moderate, and one by one the distant foghorns fell silent. *Zibaq*, going barely fast enough to make a bow-wave, chugged steadily westwards till Everett identified some faraway lights as Hastings promenade, and headed more northerly. As day broke they sighted Clifflands, its watchtower glowing a welcome, and Lynn said, "I do hope Mother hasn't sat up waiting for us."

"I left a note telling her not to," said Everett, "but you know your mother. She's probably up there now with a pair of nightglasses, trying to see how many there'll be for breakfast. I warned her that we'd have Don for certain, and with any luck Carlos too."

"You old crook," said his daughter fondly. "So you never meant it to be a mere reconnaissance at all?" Hugh Everett only smiled.

Pale sunlight lit the cliffs when at long last they crept into Furzehill Cove and angled up to the jetty. Lynn led the way up the zigzag steps, the Colonel toiling behind her and Kendrick coming third. He was feeling extremely tired, and wondering if he would ever again have two nights' sleep in succession. Urquiza, from the look of him, was in no better shape, but Lynn seemed bright as a bird; and her father, who had stayed behind to moor the boat, also looked fresh and fit as he came after them two steps at a time. A resilient family. No doubt a bouncing Mrs. Everett would meet them at the top, offering a choice of grapefruit or cereal.

It was not Mrs. Everett who met them, however, it was Manuela; but "them" gives a wrong impression, for she had eyes only for Urquiza. "Carlos, *querido*," she crooned, advancing with outstretched arms and an expression that would have seduced a statue. Slightly embarrassed, Kendrick glanced away, and was thus never able to say quite what occurred. But he heard the blood-curdling scream, saw the flailing denim-clad figure hurtle downwards, and heard the sickening sounds as it caromed off sharp rocks into the sea.

Manuela was staring after it, and in a moment her face was a mask of horror and grief. But for that one split second Kendrick had seen the savage triumph in her eyes; and he knew that, inexplicably but deliberately, the rattlesnake had struck.

POSTSCRIPT

Breakfast was not, after all, a happy meal; and there were only three at table, for upstairs in a darkened bedroom Mrs. Everett was ministering to the prostrate Manuela, who had succumbed to hysterics immediately after giving a clear and plausible account of the tragedy.

Carlos, she said, had had a sudden spasm of cramp, to which he had always been a martyr, and, doubling up in agony, had staggered back from her embrace, lost his footing and gone over the edge. Since delicacy had made Lynn, like Kendrick, look aside at the crucial moment, and since Everett had still been only halfway up the cliff-face, nobody had actually witnessed the kiss of death. But, as Manuela's determination to marry the Colonel was well known, there was no reason to think that she might have wanted him dead instead. Kendrick alone had glimpsed the giveaway in her eyes, and he did not mention it. And Hadley, who had personal experience of her clinch-breaking technique, was of course not there to comment.

The body had gone from sight with the ebbing tide, and they had made no attempt to look for it. Some day, somewhere, it would no doubt be found, but there was little chance that anyone would come forward to identify it, or that its point of origin would ever be known; for Clifflands was the only house overlooking that particular stretch, and there had been no boats within eyeshot.

The sudden disappearance of Madame Zingara might surprise a few people, but not even Inez was likely to start a "Missing Persons" search for her; for Inez had got away with one perfectly good jeep and, as they were later to discover, the considerable amount of ready cash that had been in the caravan.

So the fortune-teller would be forgotten; Carlos Urquiza, or what the sea might leave of him, would lie in a nameless grave; and Anglo-Colombian relations would continue to be cordial.

"I suppose I'd better phone the office," said Everett heavily, crumpling his napkin beside his plate, "and tell them the operation was successful but the patient died."

"This rather scuppers the London & Global expansion programme, I take it," said Kendrick. "Or can you find a replacement for Carlos?"

Everett shook his head. "Not a chance," he said. "We've got nobody else who's known beyond his own back yard, and it takes a national figure to head a breakaway. No, I'm afraid we can write-off Colombia." He went out.

Lynn turned gravely to Kendrick and said, "She pushed him over, didn't she?"

The journalist caught his breath. "Yes," he said. "Did you see her do it?"

"No, but . . . it had to be that. It explains so much—like her surprising candour about wanting to be First Lady of the republic. That's really not the kind of thing you confide to comparative strangers, so I guessed she was doing it as a screen for something else. But I never thought the something else was more sinister than the fact that she didn't care a cuss for Carlos."

"You can't have known till this morning that she didn't."

"Don, please! A woman is on her way to meet her beloved after two long years of separation, so what does she do? Tries to postpone the reunion for twentyfour hours so that she can have one more night with another man."

"That was only to recover the letter," said Kendrick uncomfortably.

Lynn smiled sardonically. "You underrate your virile charm,

dear," she said. "If she'd really been anxious about the letter she'd have asked you to take it ashore and then hand it back to her right away, outside the Customs shed. No. The dinner jacket bit was strictly eyewash, Don, to make her proposed overnight stop in Glasgow seem reasonable to Daddy and his associates. She obviously didn't give a damn what happened to the letter, and that's what I simply couldn't understand. But of course I get it now. Why should she, when she knew that the breakaway would never take place anyhow, for lack of a leader? It's apparent now that she came to England for only one reason—to catch up with Carlos and kill him. But why? It couldn't have been jealousy, could it?"

"No," said Kendrick, "it wasn't jealousy. It was revenge."

"For what?"

"Something that's been staring me in the face for two days, ever since I learned that they'd been long-time lovers; and staring your father in the face, I may add, for two years. I saw it only a few minutes ago, though, and he hasn't seen it yet."

"But what is it?"

"Carlos fled the country when his revolt failed, if you remember, saving his own hide but ditching Manuela, and leaving her to face the music. Wouldn't you feel a little murderous yourself if your lover betrayed you like that?"

Lynn nodded. "I'd want to carve him in pieces," she said.

"Carlos can't have had any illusions about it, either. That's the only thing that explains his behaviour when I found him in the yacht. He knew I knew Manuela, and he thought I was helping her to find him and avenge herself."

"Wait a minute. If he knew she'd be gunning for him, why did he go sailing into her arms when they met?"

"The male, honey, is a conceited animal. We're always ready to believe that the little woman still loves us in spite of everything. That 'Carlos, *querido*' act would certainly have fooled me, if I'd been Carlos, so no doubt it deceived him too—for the necessary couple of seconds."

Again Lynn nodded. "That's it," she agreed. "But don't ever breathe a word of it to Daddy. He's feeling sick enough already."

Leaving Lynn to help her mother with Manuela, Kendrick drove to his hotel, changed into clothes that had not been swum in, paid his bill and headed for London. He was due back in the office on Saturday, he reflected, so if he was ever going to make his flat habitable again he would have to do it in the next two and a half days. But first he would drop in at Scotland Yard, and give Antony Dane a few hints about Radio Samantha.

"Thanks," said the detective when he had finished. "Thanks very much indeed. For that, I'll try to talk Lancashire out of prosecuting you for committing a public mischief. The yacht's outside our jurisdiction, of course, but . . . useful to know about her. Oh, yes."

"Tell me something in return," said Kendrick. "When you found out that my second mysterious visitor was Hugh Everett, why didn't you even question him?"

The Chief-Inspector grinned. "For one thing," he said, "I knew that he couldn't possibly be involved with communist saboteurs. For another, I knew that he'd probably claim he'd only been checking up on the fellow his daughter was running around with. And for a third, I knew that he and the Foreign Secretary were old school chums. In this job, Don, you learn to tread delicately."

When Kendrick had left, the detective contemplated his telephone for a minute, then lifted it and called an old school chum of his own, now employed at the Admiralty as Deputy Director of Underwater Operations. For a time they talked about frogmen.

At five Kendrick's telephone rang and Lynn said, "I've found out why the Hadley party gave up the search for us so soon. Have you seen the evening papers?" He had not, so she told him that Hadley, described as a director of the Samantha company, had had an accident aboard the yacht while cleaning a .22 rifle he had not known was loaded. It had gone off, and the bullet had entered one of his lungs. He had been rushed ashore by launch and was now, after surgery, reported comfortable in the West Kent Infirmary. "I've sent him a dozen roses and a 'Get Well' card," said Lynn. "I thought it was the least I could do."

Kendrick laughed and said, "I doubt if he even knows your name, honey."

"That occurred to me," said the girl. "And then I remembered your calling me Miss Oakley just after I'd shot him, so I signed it 'Annie the Accident'."

On the forenoon of Saturday, October 4, Hugh Everett watched Manuela take off for Montreal in a jet liner, and Don Kendrick returned to Fleet Street and duty. One of the first news items he chanced on was an agency flash about a hit-and-run death in Datchet. Primo Alberdi, discharged from hospital only that morning, had been killed by a speeding car which had mounted the sidewalk. The car, a stolen one, had later been found abandoned. So the poor guy hadn't been kidding about the fate of failures.

After conferring with Quayle and the Editor, Kendrick wrote a guarded and, they hoped, non-actionable story about an unnamed radio pirate that was really only a front for foreign agents. It was a poor end-product, he felt, for something that had at one time promised so much, but it was the best he could do; until 10 p.m., when Reuters reported that Radio Samantha had been holed below the waterline by an unexplained explosion, and was sinking fast. The crew had abandoned ship.

Kendrick's story was at once re-written, much less guardedly, and the two items were run side by side. With a picture of the yacht, the latest bulletin on Hadley's health, and a sceptical rehash of the gun-cleaning story, they made quite an effective half-page.

Lynn was out dinner-dancing, Kendrick knew, so he waited till midnight before he phoned to tell her of *Samantha*'s fate. "It makes a neat little ending to that chapter in our lives," he said. "I was wondering how best to start the next one, when it struck me that Sunday's my day off and that you've not yet seen my refurbished flat. How's about coming round for breakfast again? We can go out somewhere afterwards, if the weather's decent."

"Sounds nice. What does the forecast say?"

"Heavy rain," said Kendrick happily, and heard a chuckle at the other end.

"If we must have wolves," said the girl, "by all means let's have the kind that bark a warning. All right, Don, I'll be round."